"Where are you, Fargo?"

Fargo had risked his neck enough. It was time to end it quickly. He had only ten feet to cover; three long strides and he would be on Lyndon like a falling tree. One blow to batter the shotgun aside, another to knock the man down, and it would be over. Just like that.

But George Lyndon wasn't the buffoon Fargo had assumed. For as the Trailsman shot toward him, Lyndon spun, his expensive English shotgun now rock steady and fixed on Fargo's abdomen.

"Die, you vermin!"

Fargo couldn't dodge, and there was nowhere to seek cover.

He was as good as dead.

THE
TRAILSMAN

#211

BADLANDS
BLOODBATH

by

Jon Sharpe

Ⓞ
A SIGNET BOOK

SIGNET
Published by New American Library, a division of
Penguin Putnam Inc., 375 Hudson Street,
New York, New York 10014, U.S.A.
Penguin Books Ltd, 27 Wrights Lane,
London W8 5TZ, England
Penguin Books Australia Ltd,
Ringwood, Victoria, Australia
Penguin Books Canada Ltd, 10 Alcorn Avenue,
Toronto, Ontario, Canada M4V 3B2
Penguin Books (N.Z.) Ltd, 182–190 Wairau Road,
Auckland 10, New Zealand

Penguin Books Ltd, Registered Offices:
Harmondsworth, Middlesex, England

Published by Signet, an imprint of New American Library, a division of
Penguin Putnam Inc.

First Printing, June 1999
10 9 8 7 6 5 4 3 2 1

The first chapter of this book originally appeared in *The Bush League*,
the two hundred tenth volume in this series.

Ⓟ REGISTERED TRADEMARK—MARCA REGISTRADA

Printed in the United States of America

The Trailsman

Beginnings . . . they bend the tree and they mark the man. Skye Fargo was born when he was eighteen. Terror was his midwife, vengeance his first cry. Killing spawned Skye Fargo, ruthless, cold-blooded murder. Out of the acrid smoke of gunpowder still hanging in the air, he rose, cried out a promise never forgotten.

The Trailsman they began to call him all across the West: searcher, scout, hunter, the man who could see where others only looked, his skills for hire but not his soul, the man who lived each day to the fullest, yet trailed each tomorrow. Skye Fargo, the Trailsman, and the seeker who could take the wildness of a land and the wanting of a woman and make them his own.

1861, the Badlands,
a fitting name if ever there was one. . . .

1

Death had a name.

Between the Kansas Territory to the north and Texas to the south lay a wasteland of living death known as the Badlands. It was bad country, plain and simple. There was little water, little vegetation. The soil was too poor to support crops. Stark hills and random buttes were crisscrossed by steep gullies and deep ravines, creating a maze for the unwary traveler. No one in his right mind ever went into the Badlands.

So Skye Fargo was all the more surprised when he crossed the trail of a heavily laden wagon that appeared to be doing just that. Puzzled, the big man in buckskins reined up and dismounted. His piercing lake blue eyes raked the ground.

Hoofprints left in the wagon's wake told him a cow plodded along behind it, probably tied to the gate. The tracks were similar to those of a buffalo, only smaller, the cloven hoof-mark more obvious. Added proof it was a cow came in the form of its droppings. Fargo examined them and saw that the animal was being fed dry grain regularly, a luxury denied the cow's wilder cousins.

The ruts left by the wheels were a story in themselves. Their depth showed how overburdened the wagon was. Many settlers made the mistake of packing everything they owned, from grandfather clocks to immense stoves, with the result being that their teams had to pull two to three times as much weight as they should. Many animals never made it across the plains; they collapsed and died from sheer exhaustion.

This particular wagon was a large Conestoga, not one of the

lighter prairie schooners so popular with settlers bound for a new life in the vast West. Six oxen were toiling under the hot sun to bring it to its destination. Footprints indicated the owner was walking beside the last animal on the left, which was customary.

Frowning, Fargo rose. It bothered him, these people heading into the Badlands. Maybe they were lost. Maybe they had strayed off one of the regular trails and were searching for a town. But if so, why were they traveling south instead of west? Were they on their way to Texas? It was the only explanation he could think of, yet they were going about it all wrong. No one ever took the Badlands route.

Debating what to do, Fargo forked leather. The Conestoga had gone by no more than an hour ago. He could easily catch up and warn them what they were in for, then be on his way. Clucking to the Ovaro, he started to do just that, then stopped again at the sight of a new set of tracks.

Fargo's first thought was that an Indian was shadowing the greenhorns, but the prints had been made by shod hoofs. It was a white man, on horseback, pacing the wagon. Kneeing his stallion forward, Fargo saw where the horseman had ridden in close to the man guiding the oxen, perhaps to confer, then gone back to his original position ten yards out.

To keep watch for hostiles, Fargo guessed. As seasoned travelers would do. Whoever they were, they apparently knew what they were doing. They must have a reason for venturing into the Badlands. He saw no reason to go on.

Lifting the reins, Fargo was about to resume his interrupted journey when a garish splash of bright color caught his eye. He moved closer, bending low over the pinto's side with his arm extended so he could snag an object partially hidden in the high grass.

It was a doll. A child's plaything, with floppy red curls and a cute painted face and a dress made of gingham. Tiny little cotton shoes had been added. There was even a yellow bow in the hair, a nice touch that hinted at the love the doll's maker bore the doll's owner.

There Fargo sat, a tall, muscular man, as rugged as the harsh land around him, bronzed by the sun to where he could pass for a Sioux warrior were it not for his beard, holding the dainty doll in his calloused hand. Pushing his hat brim back, he pondered. His gaze drifted to the southwest, in the general direction of Arizona, his destination. Then it swiveled to the south.

"Damn."

The Ovaro pricked its ears and twisted its neck to regard him closely. It could read his intentions almost as well as Fargo read sign. Small wonder, given how long they had been together. Fargo's wanderlust had taken them from the mighty Mississippi to the broad Pacific, from the baked deserts of Mexico to the frigid woodlands of Canada. He'd sooner part with an arm or leg than his dependable mount.

A light flick of the reins was all it took to send the pinto trotting after the Conestoga. Shifting, Fargo placed the doll in his saddlebags. The presence of a child changed everything. He had to let the party know the dangers they were letting themselves in for. Whether they heeded the warning was up to them. At least he could ride on afterward with a clear conscience.

No one had any business taking a little girl into the Badlands. If thirst didn't get them, hostiles might. Roving bands of Comanches, Kiowa, and Cheyenne passed through the region often, either hunting buffalo or on raids. Then there were the whites who haunted the desolate wilds, badmen every bit as vicious as the land itself, men on the dodge, cutthroats who would as soon dry-gulch unwary innocents as look at them.

Fargo held to a brisk pace until the grassy flatland blended into a series of low gypsum hills that marked the unofficial boundary of the Badlands. The wagon had wound in among them, but Fargo rode to the top of the highest to scout the countryside. Ahead lay blistered terrain that looked as if it had been hacked at by a giant with a gigantic hoe. Not so much as an insect stirred. No birds sang. No deer or antelope or buffalo were to be seen. The land appeared as dead as a corpse.

It didn't help any that the day was unbearably hot. By Fargo's reckoning, the temperature had to be in the upper nineties. The scorched air was as lifeless as everything else. His skin prickled as he descended to the wagon ruts and paralleled them deeper into the muggy heart of the godforsaken emptiness.

Shrub trees and scrub brush were the exception rather than the rule. Occasional tracts of dying grass offered feeble grazing. There wasn't any sign of water but Fargo wasn't worried. He was adept at finding it where most men couldn't. Yet another of the many skills that had earned him the nickname Trailsman.

Suddenly, Fargo stiffened. Wispy tendrils rose from a small valley beyond the hills. It was unlikely the pilgrims had made camp so early, so the smoke must have a more sinister source. Comanches weren't above burning the wagon and all its contents—after disposing of the occupants, of course.

Yanking his Henry from the saddle scabbard, Fargo brought the stallion to a gallop. He worked the trigger guard to lever a round into the chamber. Hugging the base of the last hill, he slowed as the valley unfolded before him. A string of cottonwoods and oaks pinpointed the location of a stream halfway across.

The smoke rose from among the trees. To reach the spot unseen, Fargo veered to the left and circled around. It delayed him but it couldn't be helped. To blunder headlong into a Comanche war party would be asking for an early grave.

Once among the cottonwoods Fargo drew rein to listen. Instead of the yips of warriors or the screams of victims, he heard faint womanish mirth.

Not taking anything for granted, Fargo advanced until movement near the stream let him know he was close enough to be seen. Sliding down, he looped the reins around a trunk. As silent as a stalking cat, he glided along until he saw a small fire. The wagon was parked in shade, the oxen and the cow grazing. A burly man in homespun clothes was inspecting the harness. Near the fire knelt a woman in a plain dress and bonnet, who was consoling a girl of about seven or eight years old.

They were perfectly fine. Fargo lowered the Henry, feeling

slightly sheepish. All the effort he had gone to on their behalf, and they behaved as if they were on a Sunday jaunt back in the States.

At the rear of the wagon another figure materialized, a lithe shape that swung to the ground in the billowy flare of a burgundy dress and a dazzling swirl of golden tresses. A woman of nineteen or twenty, a beauty who would turn the head of any man, held aloft a bundle and called out, "I found it, Ma."

"Fetch it here, Mary Beth," the woman at the fire responded. "Your sister needs something to cheer her up."

Mary Beth obeyed, a lively spring to her step, an alluring sway to her hips. High cheekbones, rosy lips, and a teardrop chin added to her loveliness. "Here you go, Claire Marie," she said to the little girl. "This will take your mind off Sally May."

Fargo idly wondered why they were so fond of saying the first and middle names. The oldest daughter handed the bundle to the mother, who promptly unwrapped a woolen swath and held out the object she uncovered.

"Remember this one, Claire Marie? You called her Patricia Jane. She was the first you ever owned."

It was another doll, smaller than the one Fargo had found, with stringy brown hair that crowned a pair of button eyes and a cross-stitched mouth. A tattered dress testified to the heavy use the doll had seen.

Claire sniffled and shook her head. "I don't want this old one, Ma! I want Sally May! She's special."

The mother sadly rested a hand on her youngest daughter's shoulder. "I'm sorry, child, but we can't go back to look for it. There's no telling where you lost it."

"You have only yourself to blame," threw in Mary Beth. "Ma told you time and time again not to sit at the very back of the wagon, that you might fall out or drop something. But you wouldn't listen."

"Now, now, Mary Beth," the mother said. "You'll only make your sister feel worse."

The girl already did. Tears welled up as Claire declared,

5

"You're mean, Mary! I didn't drop her! I think I lost her when we hit that big bump!"

Fargo could end the child's suffering. Cradling the Henry, he approached their camp. Typical of greenhorns, no one spotted him until he was almost on top of them. Then the oldest daughter, Mary Beth, looked up and gasped in alarm. Their mother leaped up, snatching the smaller girl to her bosom. All three gaped in dismay, as if he were a Kiowa painted for war.

"Who the devil are you, mister?" Mary Beth recovered her wits first.

"A friend," Fargo said.

Anxiety etched the mother's features. Tilting her head, she shouted, "Edward! Edward! There's a stranger here!"

The man pivoted. He had a square jaw, bushy brows, and hands the size of hams. Hurrying over, he mustered a wary smile, the smile of a man who had been caught with his guard down and was hoping his negligence wouldn't cost his loved ones their lives. "Howdy, friend," he said earnestly, thrusting out one of those oversized hands. "Edward Webber, at your service. This is my family."

Fargo shook, gave his name, and further put them at ease by saying, "I came across your trail a while back and was worried you might run into trouble."

"Aren't you from Paradise?" Edward asked.

"Where?"

"The town we're headed to," the settler said, then introduced the others.

The wife's name was Esther. She set Claire down once she was assured Fargo posed no threat, and said, "Would you care for some coffee? I was just about to put some on, and we'd be delighted to have you join us. Your company is most welcome. Other than Mr. Vetch, we haven't seen a living soul in weeks."

"Count yourself lucky," Fargo mentioned. "This is Indian country. If you're on your way to Texas, you're well west of where you should be."

Edward Webber shook his head. "Paradise isn't in Texas."

There was that name again. In all Fargo's wide-flung travels, he'd never heard of it. But then, new settlements were springing up all the time. "Where is it? Eastern Arizona?"

"No, no," Edward said, chuckling. "It's not more than a two-day ride from here."

"Paradise is in the *Badlands*?" Fargo couldn't keep the shock from his voice. As near as he knew, the wastelands were as empty of habitation as they were of everything else. Surely he'd have heard if a town had been started up. It would be the talk of every saloon from Denver to Santa Fe.

Edward's bushy brows knit. "What are the Badlands?"

To say Fargo was flabbergasted would not do his astonishment justice. He was well aware that far too many settlers were woefully ignorant of life in the West, but this beat all. Most never bothered to learn about the wildlife or Indians or anything else of importance. They just loaded up their belongings and traipsed off to the Promised Land with complete confidence Providence would spare them from harm.

Here was a sterling example. A man who had brought his family into one of the worst regions in the whole country, and he *didn't even know where he was*. Some people, Fargo mused, were dumber than the beasts of burden they relied on to get them where they were going. "The name speaks for itself." Fargo gestured. "And you're in them."

The eldest daughter, Mary Beth, had been listening attentively while studying Fargo on the sly. He'd noticed her admiring the width of his shoulders, and he inwardly grinned when she let her eyes linger lower down. "If that's true," she broke in, "how come Mr. Vetch never mentioned it?"

"Who is this Vetch character?" Fargo inquired.

"Cyrus Vetch," Edward Webber elaborated. "He came along when we needed him most. Our wagon had lost a wheel and I couldn't get the spare on by myself. If not for him, we'd still be stranded in the middle of the Kansas prairie."

"He's from Paradise," Mary Beth said. "The owner of the general store there. He was one of the first to stake a claim, and he's helped to make the town a thriving success."

"In the *Badlands*?" Fargo repeated. Maybe he was unwilling

7

to believe it, he reflected, because it confirmed what he had long feared. That one day settlers would swarm over the West like a plague of locusts, overrunning it with homesteads and towns and cities until there wasn't a square foot of wilderness left. All the wild beasts and the Indians and open spaces would be gone, and with them the way of life that Fargo loved.

Here was evidence it might really happen. If settlers could put down roots in the Badlands, they could put down roots *any-where*. No place was safe, not the highest peak or the remotest valley. It was the beginning of the end.

Mary Beth chuckled, a silken, throaty bubbling, like rapids over rocks, full of vitality and sensual charm. "You're a strange one, Mr. Fargo. I should think you would be glad for us. Now we don't need to go all the way to Oregon."

"That's right," her father said. "We can take our pick of prime land. Within a year I'll be plowing my own fields, storing grain in my own barn." Edward rubbed his hands in eager anticipation. "Cyrus tells us that he knows of a valley where the grass is green all year. It has a fine spring and plenty of game."

Fargo couldn't help himself from being skeptical, and gazed around the clearing. "Where is this Mr. Vetch? I'd like to meet him."

"Oh, he went off to hunt," Edward said. "We stopped a bit earlier than usual because my wife is feeling poorly. Some venison and a good night's sleep should have her fit as a fiddle by morning."

"Is she sick?" Fargo asked. Certain roots and plants were quite effective in curing aches and ills, and he was versed in their use.

"Not in the way you mean," Edward said, glancing at his wife, who was rummaging in the back of the wagon. He nodded at his oldest daughter, who had been gawking at Fargo the whole time, as if there were more he wanted to say but couldn't with her present. Fargo's confusion must have shown because Edward added, "Once a month or so we have the same problem."

Mary Beth blushed. "Pa!"

Now it was Fargo's turn to chuckle. "That's all right. I'm a grown man. You're a grown woman. What's the harm?"

Her blush deepened. Scooping up her younger sister, Mary Beth flounced toward the wagon, sniping over a shoulder, "There are some subjects that should never be talked about in front of a lady. If Ma found out, she'd blister your ears, Pa."

Edward Webber sighed. "Women. We can't live without them, and we can't live with them. What's a fellow to do?"

Fargo's chuckle became a belly laugh. He bent forward, holding his side, and in doing so he inadvertently saved his life. For as he did, a rifle cracked and a slug buzzed so close above his head that it nudged his hat. Instantly, Fargo flung himself flat, then rolled, bringing the Henry up and around with the stock pressed to his shoulder. Edward was imitating a stupefied ox. The women had frozen in amazement.

"Get down!" Fargo hollered.

The rifleman in the trees fired again. Gunsmoke puffed skyward as the bullet thudded in the earth at Fargo's elbow. He banged off two swift shots in reply, aiming at the smoke, and he must have come close because a vague shape retreated into the brush. In a twinkling, Fargo heaved upright and gave chase, bellowing at the pilgrims, "Take cover under the wagon!"

The bushwhacker was in full flight.

Fargo weaved among the cottonwoods, eager for a clear shot. He caught a glimpse of a man in buckskins. Without warning, the bushwhacker whirled and snapped off another shot, forcing Fargo to dive behind a tree. It bought the would-be killer a few precious seconds.

Swearing, Fargo pushed to his feet and resumed his pursuit. They were bearing due east, along the north bank of the stream, where cover was heaviest. Twice he almost fired, but in each instance he didn't have a clear enough shot.

Who could it be? Fargo wondered. A lone warrior out to slay a white for the sheer hell of it? Possibly, but Fargo was doubtful. Warriors generally roved in war parties, not singly. Was it a white man—a badman—then? Maybe. But, like warriors, they tended to travel in groups.

The only other prospect Fargo could think of was the mystery man, Cyrus Vetch. So far as Fargo knew, Vetch was the only other person within fifty miles. But why would Vetch try to put a window in his skull? What did the man hope to gain?

Another slug, shattering a low limb close to Fargo's right ear, put an end to his speculation. He had let his mind stray at the worst possible moment. Angry at himself, he answered in kind, not once but twice, a waste of lead since he couldn't see his target.

Feet drummed dully. Fargo closed on the sound, narrowing the gap. He was no more than forty or fifty feet from his quarry when a horse nickered. Pumping his legs faster, he spied its silhouette outlined against the background of green growth. He also saw the bushwhacker clambering onto the saddle. Again Fargo brought up the Henry, but as he fixed a hasty bead the man slapped his legs and the horse bolted around a wide oak. Thwarted, Fargo listened to the crackling and crashing fade in the distance, then he jerked his rifle down and turned on a boot heel.

The bastard had gotten clean away! Fargo was tempted to go after him, to track the man down no matter how long it took. But that would mean leaving the Webber family on their own, and he was reluctant to part company until he had learned more about Paradise—and Cyrus Vetch.

Hiking to the Ovaro, Fargo stepped into the stirrups and rode to their camp. They had done as he instructed and were huddled under the Conestoga, Edward and Esther armed with rifles, Mary Beth with the Walker Colt. Their relief at seeing him alive was genuine. They bustled out as he slid down.

Much to Fargo's surprise, Mary Beth put a warm hand on his arm and gave a soft squeeze. "Thank God you weren't hurt! All that shooting! We feared the worst."

Was her concern simple friendship or something more? Fargo couldn't say.

"Did you see who it was?" Esther wanted to know.

"A skulking savage, I'll wager," Edward declared. "Vetch warned us there are a few in this neck of the woods."

Fargo was making it a habit to repeat half of what the farmer said. "Just a few?" Tying the pinto to the wagon bed, he shoved the Henry into the scabbard. "Half the warriors in the Comanche nation pass through this area two or three times a year." He turned to his saddlebags.

Edward snorted. "Surely you exaggerate, friend. Cyrus guaranteed me the countryside around Paradise is as safe as Illinois. He told us the last Indian attacks took place over a decade ago."

Fargo wanted to say that Vetch was an idiot but he refrained. As a general rule he never insulted someone unless he could do so to his face. "I almost forgot," he said, undoing the straps. "I have something that belongs to one of you."

Claire let out with a delighted squeal when Fargo showed her the doll. She beamed and hugged it close, then startled Fargo by clasping his legs and giving him the same affectionate treatment.

"Thank you, Mr. Fargo! Thank you, thank you, thank you! Sally May is my best friend in all the world!"

Mary Beth snickered. "It's just a silly doll. But the way you carry on, a body would think it was flesh and blood."

Esther Webber pointed at her oldest. "You have no room to talk, missy. As I recall, there was a doll you were fond of when you were Claire Marie's age. Gladys, you called her, and you wouldn't go to bed at night unless she was tucked at your side."

Mary blushed again. "I didn't know any better back then. I was only a kid."

"And what do you think your sister is?" Esther countered.

Edward motioned at the fire. "How about that coffee we promised you, Mr. Fargo? We'd be honored if you'd stick around. Maybe stay the night if you're so inclined." He paused. "Besides, Mr. Vetch is bound to return before too long and you can learn all about Paradise firsthand."

Fargo's gaze drifted across the clearing, then from the father to the mother to the oldest daughter. As a Texan might say, she was as fine a filly as he had ever set eyes on, her full breasts seeming to strain against her dress like ripe fruit fit to burst.

The enticing swell of her thighs was added incentive. "I'll take you up on your offer, Ed."

The family was in fine spirits. They chattered like chipmunks, grateful that Fargo had saved them. They thought all was well, but Fargo knew better. The killer who had opened fire on them might come back—with friends.

Acting relaxed but always alert, Fargo sipped the delicious coffee Mrs. Webber made and answered a hundred and one questions about everything from the change of seasons to the migration of buffalo.

Edward, in particular, was interested in anything that had a bearing on farming. Blazing bands of red, orange, and vivid yellow painted the western sky when he stretched and commented, "The sun will be going down in half an hour. I can't imagine where Mr. Vetch has gotten to."

"What does he look like?" Fargo asked, expecting Ed to say that Vetch wore buckskins, too.

"Oh, he's a roly-poly gent with a smile that would melt butter. About the friendliest human being I've ever met. He wears store-boughten clothes, a gray jacket and pants and a white shirt. And a fancy gray bowler."

Esther tittered. "Please don't tell him I said this, but Cyrus is quite comical. He makes me think of the circus clown we saw over in Hartford that time we visited my sister."

"We're from Illinois," Ed remarked.

Fargo had already deduced as much. He was more interested in the description of their kindly benefactor. Based on their description, it couldn't possibly have been Vetch who tried to make wolf meat of him. "I'm looking forward to meeting your friend," he said, reaching for the coffeepot.

Just then, to the west, a wavering shriek fluttered on the wind, the horrified wail of someone suffering anguish beyond measure.

2

"Land sakes!" Esther Webber exclaimed, rising and snatching hold of Claire. She blanched chalk white, her throat bobbing in fright.

Edward also jumped up, his Spencer in hand. "Mercy! It sounds like someone is being tortured!"

Fargo was trying to gauge the distance. "Quiet!" he barked, cocking his head as the cry undulated eerily. It couldn't be more than a quarter of a mile. Setting down the tin cup, he hastened toward the Ovaro. The Webbers flocked around him as if for protection, Mary Beth so close her elbow brushed his. "Keep your guns handy until I get back."

The blonde blinked. "You're not going to leave us alone?"

"Someone has to go," Fargo responded, although he didn't want to any more than she wanted him to. "It might be your friend, Cyrus Vetch." No one else protested as he mounted.

The wail finally died. Fargo touched his spurs to the stallion, bearing westward. The sun was perched on the rim of the world, casting the Badlands in ever-lengthening shadows except for the crests of the gypsum hills, which seemed to glow with an unearthly light. Fargo rode at a canter until he judged he was near where the cry had originated. He hoped it would be repeated, but the Badlands mocked him with its usual stillness.

Once among the hills, Fargo suddenly had the feeling he was being watched. Never one to discount his intuition, he drew rein and scoured the vicinity. *Nothing*. Palming his Colt, he went cautiously on.

Another minute elapsed. The skin between his shoulder blades began to itch, as it had that time Apaches had jumped him in the Dragoons. Swiveling, Fargo probed the slopes behind him, but saw nothing to account for the sensation.

He continued deeper into the hills. It made no sense, none of this. The attempt on his life. Now the terrible scream. Were they somehow related?

Fargo shook his head to derail his train of thought so he wouldn't make the same mistake he had earlier going after the bushwhacker. He must concentrate on what he was doing to the exclusion of all else. As if to stress the point, a strident screech whipped his gaze overhead. But it was only a solitary red hawk, wheeling high in the sky. The bird of prey was the first sign of life Fargo had seen, and he marveled that it could find enough to eat in these wastelands. The hawk screeched again, as if upset at having an intruder in its domain, then it banked and sailed majestically off.

A clattering noise brought Fargo down to earth. It came from beyond the next hill. Slowing even more, he thumbed back the Colt's hammer. Every nerve was on edge as he climbed to within ten yards of the crest, slid down, and bellied to the rim. Removing his hat, he poked his head up high enough to see what lay on the other side.

More hills. That was all. Nothing moved in the gathering gloom save for a snake. A rattler, Fargo thought, but it slid under a boulder and was gone before he could be sure. He figured the reptile had dislodged some stones as it glided along.

By now the sun had partially dipped from sight. Another ten minutes and it would be gone. To take advantage of the remaining light, Fargo climbed back on the pinto and descended.

If he didn't know better, Fargo would swear someone had deliberately lured him away from the Webbers. But no gunshots had blasted back at the stream, so it wasn't a ploy to slay them. Whoever was responsible had something else up his sleeve.

Fargo came to the bottom and trotted between two windworn hills littered with large boulders. Their sides were steeper than most, the pair so close together he felt hemmed in. He had gone a score of yards when he spotted wisps of dust hovering like tiny ghosts above the slope on his right. It occurred to him that this was where the stones had been dislodged. And as the insight dawned, so did an urgent question. If the snake wasn't to blame, what was? Or, rather, *who* was?

Fargo heard a shuffling sound, high up above the boulders. He saw a shadowy form and raised the Colt, but it disappeared. Quickly, he reined the Ovaro onto the hill. The next moment a boulder the size of a calf came loose and careened downward. It crashed into others, dislodging them, much like a cue ball hitting other billiard balls, and in a span of seconds several tons of hurtling rock were tumbling lower, toward the bottom of the hill—and Fargo.

Hauling on the pinto's reins, the Trailsman fled for his life. In his ears pealed thunderous doom. The whole top layer of the hill was in motion, a layer of loose talus which had only needed the right spark to set it off. Or the right leverage.

Cackling glee from on high was like salt on Fargo's wounded pride. He had blundered into the trap like a rank tenderfoot. He would be crushed, smashed to a pulp, him and the stallion both, and all because he hadn't trusted his instincts.

Years of life in the wild, of dealing daily with razor claws, savage fangs, cold steel, and hot lead had honed a sixth sense in Fargo that seldom failed him. The same uncanny sense wild animals possessed. He knew better than to ignore it. Whenever he did, he paid dearly. As he might now.

The Ovaro fairly flew without Fargo having to spur it on. They pounded toward open ground and safety, as all around them stones and larger rocks and boulders rained down in a deluge. One stung Fargo's cheek. Another numbed his left wrist. The stallion whinnied when a rock struck its flank but it didn't slacken its pace.

The din was nigh deafening. Fargo had the illusion the whole world was crashing down on top of them. The little light remaining was blotted out by the thick earthen downpour. Dust choked his nose, his lungs. It filled his eyes, stinging them, making them water. It caked his clothes and his saddle.

All of which Fargo barely noticed. Tucked at the waist, he rode like a madman. A boulder as big as a strongbox slammed into the soil with a retort as loud as a cannon. Another rock, big enough to crush the Ovaro like a twig, flashed past in front of them, missing the pinto by an arm's length.

The demented glee above faded. Fargo imagined the culprit was waiting with baited breath to see if the trap succeeded. A jagged stone smacked Fargo's shoulder, ripping the buckskin, another doing the same to his leg. Out of the corner of his left eye he saw another enormous boulder rumbling toward him, the hugest yet, a boulder as immense as a bull buffalo. Were it to strike them, it would grind their bones to powder.

"Go, boy! Go!" Fargo urged, using his spurs.

The onrushing boulder made as much noise as a runaway steam engine. It loomed larger and larger until it was so close, Fargo could have turned and touched it. Another bound by the Ovaro, though, and they were in the clear.

The boulder rolled across the spot they had just occupied, clipping the stallion's tail.

More loose stones and dust swirled as thick as flies but they were safe, beyond the worst of the slide. Fargo streaked another twenty yards, then cut to the left and swung on around the hill to come up on the man responsible unseen. Two could play at the man's game, and this time Fargo wasn't letting him get away.

The boom of falling talus went on and on, muffling Fargo's ascent. Instead of dismounting and scaling the crown on foot, he charged up and over, his Colt out and extended. But there was no one to shoot. He drew rein in frustrated fury, staring at the last of the cascading debris.

Fargo surveyed the hills. The son of a bitch was nowhere to be seen. Encroaching darkness cloaked the lower slopes and washes in premature night. An army could be hidden down there and he wouldn't know it.

"This makes twice," Fargo fumed. About to go back down,

he spied an oak branch lying beside a cavity where a boulder had been. The nearest trees were those along the stream, so whoever started the avalanche had brought the limb for that express purpose. Was it the same man who had tried to blow his head off? The killer in buckskins? Or was it someone else?

Racked by questions he couldn't answer, Fargo made a beeline for the Webbers. When he was still an arrow's flight from their camp he noticed a dun tied to the wagon and a man dressed mainly in gray seated at the fire with the family.

The Webbers jumped up as he came into the flickering glow and ran to meet him.

"Fargo!" Edward said. "We were getting worried."

The wife shared her husband's sentiments. "We heard the most peculiar sound. Mr. Vetch thought it might be an explosion."

Mary Beth rested her hand on Fargo's leg and showed her white, even teeth. "I had half a mind to go search for you, but Pa wouldn't let me. He said you can take care of yourself."

Fargo was scrutinizing Cyrus Vetch. The store owner was every bit as plump as Mrs. Webber had claimed. Thick jowls, a double chin, and a bulbous nose contrived to give him a perennially friendly expression.

The pudgy man rose, doffing his bowler. "Howdy, stranger! Glad to see you're alive. These fine folks were greatly disturbed. They've sure taken a liking to you."

"How long have you been here?" Fargo demanded.

Vetch acted confused. "I don't understand—"

"How long?" Fargo pressed him.

Esther Webber wagged a finger. "Honestly, Mr. Fargo, you have the most suspicious disposition. Mr. Vetch showed up not ten minutes after you left and he's been here with us ever since."

"That's gospel," Edward confirmed.

Cyrus Vetch chortled good-naturedly. "Don't tell me. You think I'm to blame for the attack this afternoon? And for whatever happened to you just a while ago?" The roly-poly man's

17

ample stomach rippled like soft dough. "What possible motive would I have, sir? The idea is ridiculous."

Fargo now thought so himself. Vetch impressed him as being about as dangerous as a loaf of bread. "I guess it is," Fargo agreed, halting at the Conestoga. Wearily, he swung down and removed his own hat. "Stand back," he advised as he swiped at the dust coating his buckskins. "Someone tried to murder me," he recounted, "by rolling boulders down on my head."

The Webber clan pestered him to learn more, so over a hot cup of coffee Fargo satisfied their curiosity. Edward and Esther were overjoyed at his narrow escape. Mary Beth sat entranced, hanging on every word. Claire, her precious doll hugged tight, dozed in her mother's lap.

Cyrus Vetch lost some of his jovial mood, and when Fargo was done, he commented, "I say, that's just awful. It goes to show that it will be a good while yet before all the riffraff are run out of this region." He faced Edward. "I suppose I haven't been as forthcoming as I should have. This area has a nasty reputation, Mr. Webber. Justly deserved, I'm afraid."

"It's called the Badlands," Ed said.

"How did you—?" Vetch said, then glanced at Fargo. "Ah, yes. Well, many people still call it that. But in a few short years their opinion will change. Once they learn about Paradise, and how vigilant we are in making our community safe for the families who settle there, people will stop saying bad things about the territory."

Fargo placed his elbows on his knees. "It's true, then? You've actually gone and started a town in the middle of the Badlands?"

"Why do you sound so stunned, sir? Surely you've heard that beauty is in the eye of the beholder? Some people like to live in the mountains, some are partial to desert country, others won't live anywhere but near the sea." Vetch leaned back and folded his hands behind his head. "I fell in love with the Badlands the first time I set eyes on it. Something about these glassy hills and glossy gulches struck a chord in my soul, and I resolved to live here the rest of my life."

18

"In the Badlands," Fargo said, more to himself than anyone else.

Vetch misconstrued. "It's not as horrible as you make it out to be. There are a few nice valleys with ample water. Paradise is located in one, and soon it will be a thriving town to rival any in Kansas or Texas."

Fargo wished he had whiskey instead of coffee. He felt like getting so drunk he couldn't see straight. It would blunt the distress of his nightmare coming true. "How many people live there now?"

"At last count I believe it was twenty-seven. That's not many, granted, but with more fine folks like the Webbers arriving every month, we're growing by leaps and bounds."

"The Comanches don't bother you?"

"They did, until I struck a bargain through a scruffy old trader. In exchange for fifty head of cattle a year and some trinkets, they've promised to leave us alone. Ten Bears himself gave me his solemn vow to that effect."

Edward was adding a log to the fire. "Who's he? An important chief?"

Fargo answered for Vetch. "Ten Bears is the leader of the Yamparika Comanches, one of the most powerful Comanche bands. His word is law. If he says the tribe won't molest anyone around Paradise, they won't. Your homestead will be safe."

"Isn't that wonderful!" Ed declared.

"Wonderful," Fargo echoed absently.

Cyrus Vetch thought so. "And since the Kiowas are allies of the Comanches, and they both have a treaty with the Cheyenne and Arapahoe, we don't have anything to fear from them, either."

Esther cleared her throat. "What about Apaches? We've heard abominable stories of the atrocities they commit."

"Put your mind at ease, Mrs. Webber. As I'm sure Mr. Fargo will verify, the Apaches dwell far to the southwest, in parts of Arizona and New Mexico. They never come this far east."

"True," Fargo confirmed, feeling more and more despondent. There was nothing to stop settlers from streaming into the

Badlands. Or was there? "You have it all worked out," he complimented Vetch, "but how will you deal with the hard cases who come here to hide out?"

"They'll stop coming once word of our vigilance committee spreads," the pudgy man said. "We've posted signs warning that anyone who commits a crime will be duly caught and formally hung. The law of the rope is the only law their type respect."

Fargo bleakly polished off the last of his coffee. Cyrus Vetch had it all worked out. Paradise couldn't help but succeed. Eventually, the whole West would be under the plow. As much as he hated to admit it, the days of the scout and frontiersman were numbered. It was as dismal a proposition as could be. He almost asked if Ed had a flask stashed somewhere in the wagon.

Vetch was staring at him. "Mr. Webber told me of your misgivings, sir. Do you still harbor them? Or have I proven beyond reproach that I take my venture seriously?"

"You're doing all that can be done," Fargo conceded.

"Paradise means everything to me. In ten years or so I expect the Badlands to become part of a new state. With some politicking, I might be able to arrange for my town to become the capital. And who knows? It wouldn't take much arm-bending to persuade me to run for governor."

Fargo secretly yearned for a Comanche to pop out of the woods and shoot Paradise's founder dead. The town's population was less than thirty people, and already Vetch saw himself in the governor's chair! Next the man would announce he planned to run for president. It was too ridiculous for words.

"What's wrong, Skye?" Mary Beth asked. "You seem upset."

"I'm just tired," Fargo fibbed.

Esther clasped her hands together. "Oh, don't tell me you're ready to turn in so early? I was hoping to hear about some of the places you've been to. Didn't you mention Denver earlier? What are the ladies wearing there? Have you seen any of the new bonnets? I hear they have ribbons in front *and* back."

For the next forty-five minutes Fargo regaled his hosts with the latest in female fashion. It was the final indignity. Yet deep down, he didn't mind. News on the frontier was hard to come by. The fairer sex had it even tougher than men in that the information and gossip they craved was as scarce as women themselves were. Sharing what little he knew was his way of repaying Esther for her kindness. And it gave Mary Beth an excuse to squirm closer to him, close enough for him to inhale her tantalizing scent with every breath.

Presently, Esther announced it was time for her and her daughters to call it a day. "I want to thank you, Mr. Fargo, most sincerely. If you should ever be in a dry-goods store and think of it, I would be grateful if you would send me one of the latest catalogs."

"Esther!" Ed said. "We can't impose on the man like that."

"It might take forever to reach you," Fargo noted.

Cyrus Vetch had an answer for everything. "Not if you mail it to her care of the Overland Stage Office in Denver. Every three or four months I have a courier pick up our mail there and bring it to Paradise. That will have to do, I'm afraid, until regular service is established."

The ladies retired to the wagon with Claire. Edward and Cyrus chatted awhile about the cost of grain and whether Ed should trade some of his oxen for horses once he arrived in Paradise. Then they spread out blankets near the fire.

Fargo arranged his own bedding close to where the animals were tethered. Two attempts on his life in one day had been enough. If there was to be a third, he would make it as hard on the killer as he could. Holding the Colt in his right hand and a new Arkansas toothpick, a slim, razor-sharp handled blade in his left, Fargo lay propped on his saddle.

A pale circle blossomed at the rear of the wagon, gazing down at him. Fargo grinned, and Mary Beth ducked back inside.

The truth be known, Fargo liked the Webbers. Really liked them. Yes, they were homesteaders. Yes, they were as green as grass. And yes, a horde of pilgrims just like them threatened to one day destroy the life he cherished. But they were good people. Generous. All they asked out of life was a roof over their

21

heads and food on their table, and all they asked of others was to be left to live in peace. He sincerely hoped settling in Paradise was the answer to their prayers.

The night passed uneventfully.

Fargo was up before any of the others, the Ovaro saddled and the fire rekindled by the time Ed stirred and sat up smacking his lips and scratching the stubble on his chin.

"Morning, Skye. The early bird gets the first cup, eh?"

Fargo smirked. "Something like that. I'll be heading out soon. There's no need to wake the others."

"Mary Beth and Claire will be terribly disappointed. They've taken a powerful shine to you. Even Esther thinks you're a fine gentleman. Her exact words."

A small lump swelled in Fargo's throat. "Is that a fact? Well, tell them I wish them the best. Maybe I'll stop by your farm one day to see how well you're doing."

"You're always welcome at our house."

Fargo shifted and saw Cyrus Vetch peering at him from under a blanket. Spying on him would be more like it, but he gave Vetch the benefit of the doubt. "Take good care of my friends. I won't take it kindly if something happens to them."

"I take good care of all the people who settle in Paradise," the man in gray said, sitting up. "We're a close-knit community. We have to be, isolated as we are. So we look out for one another. Mark my words. They'll be fine."

"How often do you have supplies brought in?" Fargo casually inquired.

Vetch sat up and rubbed his balding pate. "Every six months or so. Why?"

"The only wagon tracks I saw were theirs," Fargo said, nodding at the Conestoga.

"Oh, that." Vetch shook himself like a bear rousing from hibernation. "Most of our provisions are brought in by mule train. It's not practical to rely on freight wagons with all these hills." He pulled his bowler from under the blanket. "But if you looked long enough, you would find where other settlers have come to Paradise from all different points of the compass."

Fargo treated himself to a cup of coffee laced with sugar, the last thing he would drink or eat all day. He had a lot of ground to make up in order to reach Tucson by the end of the week, so he wasn't going to stop again until nightfall.

Ed Webber rose onto his knees. "Frankly, Mr. Vetch, I'm glad we ran into you. I wasn't looking forward to the long trek to Oregon. A friend of mine made the journey last year, and he wrote us to say his family was lucky to reach the Willamette Valley alive."

"It's an arduous ordeal," Vetch said. "Hostiles, drought, storms, and flash floods, they all take their toll. By diverting to Paradise, you've spared your loved ones untold hardship. I commend you."

Fargo had to hand it to Vetch. The man would make a great patent-medicine salesman. Suddenly he wanted to be shed of the Good Samaritan's company. Gulping the coffee, he straightened and arched his spine to relieve a kink. "I'll circle the valley before I leave in case the polecat who bushwhacked me is still around."

"Can't you stay a little longer?" Ed requested. "You'll break Claire's heart if you don't say good-bye. Ever since you saved her doll, she sees you as her guardian angel."

"I lost my wings long ago," Fargo said dryly.

Ed grinned. "But you know how kids are. Esther has been reading to them from the Bible every night, and Claire just loves angels."

Fargo held out his hand. "Take care."

"Go with God."

After a curt nod to Cyrus Vetch, Fargo made for his stallion. A twinge of guilt gnawed at him like a beaver at a tree. He felt as if he were abandoning the Webbers, deserting them when they were in need, but that was silly. Two attempts had been made on *his* life, not on theirs. So long as he stayed, he put their lives in peril. By going off alone, he'd draw the killer away. Or so he hoped.

23

The pinto was waiting with head high. Fargo stroked its neck, saying softly, "I need this like a grizzly needs a hip pocket." Then, grasping the reins, he started to hike his right foot.

"You'd really leave without saying so long?"

Mary Beth wore a loose-fitting robe that did little to conceal her maidenly charms. Her cleavage spilled over the top like twin melons, and the lower half of her shapely left leg was exposed. Sleep had disheveled her silken yellow hair, but instead of dampening her allure, the golden tangle heightened it.

"I thought you were asleep," Fargo said, the hurt in her eyes searing him like red-hot pokers.

"So you just sneak off? I realize we hardly know each other, but I thought—" Mary Beth caught herself and took a step back. "I guess I've misjudged you."

"I'm not looking to step into any woman's loop," Fargo justified himself. "If that's what you're thinking."

Mary Beth opened her mouth to say more but Claire Marie picked that moment to hustle up to them. Like her older sister, she wore a robe, only hers was two sizes too big and covered her like a tent.

"Mr. Fargo? You're going so soon?"

"Afraid so, little one." Fargo patted her doll's red curls. "Watch out for Sally May. You wouldn't want to lose her a second time."

"We like you a whole lot. I wish you'd stay," the girl said with the frankness typical of children everywhere.

The saddle creaked as Fargo straddled the hurricane deck. "If I could, I would. But you're better off going on to Paradise without me."

"If you say so," Claire said, her tone telling him she didn't believe it for one second. "Will we ever see you again?"

"Count on it."

Fargo wheeled the stallion and crossed the clearing. Esther had climbed down and was flanked by her daughters, all three so sorrowful they looked as if they were losing their best

24

friend. Edward was frowning. Only Cyrus Vetch waved cheerfully.

Annoyed, Fargo goaded the pinto into a trot. He was doing the right thing. He was sure of it. So why was he so damn miserable? Shutting them from his thoughts, he squared his shoulders. He had a killer to catch.

3

It was only ten in the morning, by Skye Fargo's reckoning, and the heat was stifling. The flat boulder on which he lay was hot enough to cook eggs. He had to fold his arms so his hands rested on his sleeves rather than on the stone surface. Behind him, the Ovaro shifted in the shade of an overhang. Below them, passing directly under the shelf they were on, was the game trail he had followed into the gypsum hills from the valley where he had left the Webbers.

Fargo was beginning to think he had made a mistake. His ploy hadn't worked. He had been lying there for over an hour but there had been no sign of the bushwhacker. Evidently he had misjudged. The man wasn't out to kill him and him alone. Debating whether to check on the settlers, he began to turn.

The stallion's ears were pricked. Fargo listened intently, and in a few moments he heard what the stallion heard; the faint clomp of hooves coming closer. Flattening again, he glued his gaze to a point in the trail where a rider was likely to first appear. Sure enough, within a minute, a lanky scarecrow in buckskins came around the bend, head bent to read sign.

Fargo's right hand slid to the Henry. The barrel was unbearably hot but he picked it up anyway. With the patience of a mountain lion, he waited as the man climbed toward him. At that range Fargo could put a slug into either of the killer's eyes with no difficulty, but he wanted the man alive to answer questions.

The scarecrow was a cautious cuss. Again and again he

scanned the slope, his dark eyes darting every which way, his right hand resting on the butt of a Remington. He had bony features, like a skull with skin, and tufts of hair on his chin rather than a full beard, much like a goat.

Fargo didn't move a muscle. Any motion, however slight, would give him away. Mentally, he marked the spot where he had left his little surprise and tensed as the rider drew near it.

Suddenly the scarecrow reined up. He'd seen the circle of small rocks Fargo had left in the middle of the trail, approximately twenty feet from the shelf. Out flashed the Remington. Perplexed, the gunman swiveled in the saddle, then glanced at the circle of rocks.

Fargo could practically read the man's thoughts. The marker had no business being there. The killer would know Fargo had made it but would be stumped as to why. Curiosity would prove his undoing; the cutthroat would want a closer look, and once he dismounted, Fargo had him.

Nudging the bay, the bushwhacker rose in the stirrups to peer into every nook and cleft he passed. He was taking no chances, this one. The Ovaro's tracks momentarily interested him. He was confirming they had been made over an hour ago, deciding that Fargo was long gone. Little did he know.

The bay halted at the circle. Quietly, the man slid off and hunkered to examine it. He touched several of the rocks, lifted them, placed them back where they had been. "What the hell does this mean?" he said to the horse.

Fargo slid the Henry over the edge and centered the sights on the man's scrawny chest. "It means you're an idiot."

The man's reflexes were cat-quick. Instantly, he threw himself to the left and brought up the Remington. But in the split second it took him to pinpoint Fargo, the Henry boomed. The slug seared into the scarecrow's right shoulder and slammed him to the earth.

Levering another round into the breech, Fargo trained the rifle on the bushwhacker's head. "Drop your hogleg or die."

A scarlet stain was spreading across the man's shirt. He attempted to rise, fell back, then groaned. "Damn you."

"I won't tell you again," Fargo said.

The killer limply tossed his revolver aside in disgust. Radiating hatred, he glared as Fargo rose, stepped to the edge of the shelf, and dropped twelve feet to the trail. "Think you're pretty clever, don't you, bastard?"

Fargo had tucked his knees to absorb the shock of landing. Unfurling, he kicked the Remington further away. "As clever as you were with that rock slide yesterday."

"I almost got you. Twice," the man boasted.

"Why?"

The bushwhacker's thin lips pinched together.

"Who are you?" Fargo demanded.

The man just sneered.

"You must have the idea you don't need to answer me. That you have a choice. You're wrong." So saying, Fargo took a short step and kicked the man in the shoulder, planting the tip of his boot on the wound. It elicited a strangled yelp and the scarecrow doubled over in agony. "I'll only ask each question once," Fargo said. "Pretend you're a clam and I'll pretend I'm a buffalo and stomp you silly."

"You bastard! You stinking bastard!" the man rolled back and forth with spittle flecking his chin.

Fargo was in no hurry. He bided his time until the killer stopped thrashing and sluggishly sat up. "I want your name."

"Sanders."

"Your full name."

"Hiram Sanders. Happy now?"

"Why did you try to put bullets and rocks through my skull?"

Sanders adopted a sullen air. "I ain't saying. Go ahead and kick me all you want, but you won't get it out of me."

"We'll see about that," Fargo said, and brought his right boot crashing down on the scarecrow's leg. Sanders howled, but that was only the start. Fargo kicked him twice, once in the ribs and once in the shoulder. Sanders flopped about on his back, his face contorted in pain.

"I'll kill you yet! So help me, I will!"

"With a busted leg?" Fargo responded, slamming his heel down on it again. Sanders arched upward as if trying to take wing, then clutched himself and cursed a mean streak. "I can do this all day," Fargo remarked when the torrent of swearing ended. "It's up to you."

"You wouldn't be so high and mighty if you weren't holding that rifle," Sanders rasped.

"But I am," Fargo said, and to emphasize the point, he drove the heavy stock against the gunman's temple. Sanders flopped over and lay still, blood trickling from a wide gash.

Stepping to a boulder half his height, Fargo squatted in its shade. He untied his bandanna and mopped his brow and neck. As he folded the bandanna to replace it, a small lizard scuttled into view. It tilted its triangular head, studying him, and immediately scuttled off.

Hiram Sanders stirred. He was a long time sitting up. Glowering like a rabid wolf, he snarled, "I'm sick and tired of you pounding on me, mister."

"I'll do it again if you don't cooperate."

"I don't reckon you'd let me have my pistol so we could settle this proper? Man to man?" When Fargo didn't answer, Sanders said, "Hell, you've got an edge. My wing feels broke." He sought to raise his right arm but couldn't. Or else he was putting on a show to get Fargo to lower his guard.

"Do you think I shed my diapers yesterday?" Fargo demanded. "Now, we'll try this again. Why did you try to kill me?"

Sanders' mouth scrunched up, as if he desired to take a bite out of his tormentor. He hesitated, until Fargo took a step toward him. "All right! All right! I'll tell you anything you want."

"Quit stalling, then."

The scarecrow grimaced. "I wanted to rob you. I was hoping you had some money on you. And some grub. I've been wandering the Badlands for a couple of weeks now, and I'm about out."

"You're by yourself?"

"What of it? I had to light a shuck out of Texas when I got into a shooting scrape with a cardsharp. The sheriff set out after me with a posse."

"For shooting a cheat?"

"Do you have any idea how thin saloon walls are? The bullet went clean through him, then through a wall, and hit a woman who was walking by. She just happened to be the sheriff's kin."

The story could be true. But *was* it? Fargo pegged the bushwhacker as the sort of man who would lie through his teeth without batting an eye. "Why stick around here? Why not go on to Kansas or Denver?"

Hiram Sanders shrugged. "I figured to lay low for a while in case that tin star sent word to lawdogs in other territories to keep their eyes skinned for me." He sat up. "In another week or so I aimed to head for California. A man can lose himself there easy, I hear tell."

"So you're working alone?"

"How many times do I have to say the same thing? It's just me, mister. No one else. I'm not part of any gang, if that's what you're thinking." Sanders shifted to make himself more comfortable, and in doing so he brought his knees close to his chest.

Fargo still wasn't entirely convinced. "Why me? Why didn't you go after one of the Webbers?"

"Is that their name? Hell, when I took that shot, I thought you were one of them. All that shrieking I did later was to draw one of you into my trap. I didn't care which one it was." Sanders' left hand slowly dipped toward his foot.

Fargo lowered the Henry to his side. "You were spying on us this morning and saw me leave. So you figured you would stalk me and finish what you started, probably when I made camp tonight."

"That's it, more or less," Sanders said. His left hand was poised above his boot. "Now what? Do you shoot me in cold blood?"

"I doubt I'll have to."

"You won't, if you'll just let me ride off. I give you my solemn word not to bother you again." Sanders casually hooked a finger into the boot. "Better yet, I promise to mend my ways. I'll walk the straight and narrow from here on out." Two more fingers disappeared.

Fargo offered no comment. There was no need. The killer had made his decision and must accept the consequences of his actions.

"It's not as if I'm a badman or anything," Sanders babbled on. "This is the first time I've ever been in trouble with the law, except for that night I got drunk and shot out some street-lamps. But hell, we all need to bay at the moon now and then."

"You picked the wrong man," Fargo said.

Sanders misunderstood. "That I did. You have more grit than most. If it had been that Webber feller, I'd likely be standing over him right now instead of the other way around." His left hand started to slide up out of the boot. "Life's strange that way. Just when you reckon you have it licked, it turns on you like a sidewinder."

"I'm not going to bury you, you know."

"What?" Sanders froze.

"The buzzards will peck out your eyes, the coyotes will feast on your guts. And you'll lie there until you rot."

Sanders understood, then, but he was committed. "I don't rightly recollect ever hating anyone, hombre, as much as I hate you." For the longest while he sat there, staring at the Henry. "Oh, hell," he declared at length. "If I can't beat a man holding a rifle, I don't deserve to live." His hand whisked out, his fingers wrapped around a derringer.

Fargo was faster. His rifle leaped up, the muzzle not more than a foot from the killer's forehead when it went off. Jolted onto his back, Hiram Sanders convulsed violently, the der-ringer hopping in his open hand like a frog. Shock widened his eyes as they locked on Fargo. "I keep a knife in my boot. I knew what you were up to."

"I—I—really hate—" Sanders croaked, and died.

Gunsmoke curled from the Henry. Fargo blew on the end of the barrel, then added a fresh cartridge. He palmed the derringer. Delving into the scarecrow's pockets, he was surprised to discover a thick roll of bills. Sanders had lied to him about needing money. What else had been a lie? Fargo also found a small jackknife and a folded sheet of paper.

The latter turned out to be a letter from "Aunt Harriet." There was no return address. It read, in part, "I'm so happy to hear you've secured a nice job at last. Your new boss sounds like an endearing man. I do hope you'll try your best and make something of yourself. Or do you take perverse delight in being the black sheep of our family? Your sainted mother would roll over in her grave if she knew all the things you done, Hiram. She always raised you to do right. Never forget that." Fargo put the letter back in the gunman's front pocket.

The bay was nearby. It hadn't bolted at the shots, but it shied when Fargo approached. He lunged, missing the reins by a fraction. Mane flying, the horse sped on down the trail and around the bend.

Delaying just long enough to grab the Remington, Fargo ran to the Ovaro. Chasing the bay in that sweltering heat wasn't to his liking, but the animal wouldn't last long on its own. He galloped to the bend and saw the other horse hundreds of yards away, in full flight. Pulling his hat brim low, Fargo galloped after it. He was resigned to a long chase but fate dictated otherwise.

The bay abruptly nickered and catapulted into a disjointed roll, coming to rest on its side in a spray of dirt. Frantically the horse attempted to rise, squealing horribly when it brought weight to bear on its front legs. Collapsing, it pitched wildly about like an upended turtle.

Fargo had a grim foreboding of what had happened. He was right. Splotches of blood led from a long-empty prairie dog hole to the stricken mount, and gleaming slivers of bone jutted from its ruptured foreleg. The limb had been shattered beyond repair.

There was only one thing to do. Either that, or let the horse slowly waste away from starvation and thirst—or be devoured alive by scavengers. Climbing down, Fargo tried to get closer but the terrified animal wouldn't let him. Avoiding a flailing hoof, he drew his Colt. "I'm sorry," he said simply. "If there were another way—"

The crisp crack of the shot spooked a rabbit hiding in dry brush. In great vaulting jumps it angled into the grass. At the apex of the next leap a slug caught it below the ear, and Fargo's supper smacked the ground like a wet cloth.

He put the rabbit to one side and set to work stripping the saddle off the bay. He had to tug and yank to drag the stirrup and cinch out from underneath the dead horse. He didn't know what he would find in the saddlebags, and he was taken aback when he saw what they contained.

"What the hell?" Fargo blurted as he pulled out a bundle of silverware wrapped in rawhide. Sterling silver, every last fork, knife, and spoon. Next was a small leather pouch that held four pocket watches. All were in perfect condition, three gold-plated, one with a solid silver case. Where had a hard case like Sanders gotten his hands on them? Fargo wondered. A jar crammed with coins was at the bottom, a couple of hundred dollars worth, all told. In the other saddlebag was jerky, a change of socks, and four knives in excellent condition; a bowie, a Green River skinner, and two butcher knives.

Mystified, Fargo stuffed everything back inside and closed the saddlebags. He threw them on the Ovaro, tying them behind his own, into which he crammed the Remington and the rabbit. Sanders had also owned a Spencer, which Fargo shoved into his bedroll.

By now it was close to eleven o'clock, and the Webbers must be well on their way to Paradise. Fargo toyed with the notion of overtaking them and giving them the money and the silverware. But parting company had caused them so much misery, he was loath to inflict himself on them again. Little Claire might bawl her heart out were he to leave them a second time.

Fargo headed northwest. The family could get by quite

nicely on their own now that they were safe from Sanders. Fargo had a hunch the cutthroat had been preying on settlers for quite some time, murdering them and taking their valuables. He would turn over the items he had found to the marshal in Tucson. Maybe relatives of the rightful owners could be tracked down.

It felt good to be on the go again. Fargo had not been to Arizona in a while, and he looked forward to hunting down old friends. To reach Tucson that much sooner, he had been cutting across country rather than taking the stage route, which was why he had stumbled on the Conestoga's tracks in the middle of nowhere.

By the middle of the afternoon the gypsum hills were dwindling. A grassy plain hundreds of miles in length would eventually bring Fargo to Apache Pass, the gateway to the land of Cochise and Mangas Coloradas.

Fargo could never say what made him turn and look over a shoulder. He had no idea anyone was following him until he saw a glimmer of sunlight off metal. It might be Indians, or even one of Sanders' friends. He rode on as if he hadn't noticed, and when another hill screened him, he galloped due north half a mile to a rare wooded tract.

As the old saw went, if it wasn't one thing, it was another. Fargo hid the stallion in some saplings and positioned himself at the edge of a thicket. He didn't count on having to wait long but it was another thirty minutes before a lone horseman neared the trees. Fargo crouched lower.

The rider was an elderly white man in a store-bought suit that had seen better days, and a hat with a short brim. The sorrel he was on was as tired as a horse could be without caving in from exhaustion. Both had enough dust on them to gag an elk. In the man's left hand was a shotgun, an expensive English model with an elaborately tooled stock and intricately engraved double barrels. Not a type of gun common on the frontier.

Fargo took him for a partner of Sanders, thirsting for revenge. Another callous killer of innocents who deserved no mercy. He wedged the Henry against his shoulder.

The elderly man had slowed to a walk. His face was haggard, as if he had gone quite a spell without much food or sleep, and the makings of a sandy beard covered his jutting chin. Thumbing back the hammers on both barrels, he braced the shotgun against his side.

Not that it would do him any good. A shotgun was only effective at short range, and Fargo wasn't going to permit the man to get close enough to use it.

At the tree line the rider reined up, then cupped a hand to his mouth. "I know you're in there, you rotten murderer! Come out with your hands where I can see them!"

Fargo raised his chin from the Henry. Were all the people in the Badlands loco, or was it him?

"I found that fellow you killed," the man called out. "And the bay you shot. So you must be the one I'm after. Tell me what you did to them or you'll never leave here alive."

There were days, Fargo reflected, when it wasn't worth the while to wake up. Rather than reply and have a load of buckshot flung in his direction, he crept around the thicket and snaked wide to the right.

"My name is Lyndon. George Lyndon. Sound familiar to you?"

Fargo didn't know the man from Moses, but he wasn't about to say a thing until he had the upper hand.

"You murdered them, you vermin! Just like you've done so many others. How many is it now, exactly? Thirty? Forty? How can you sleep at night with so many souls to account for? How?"

The man's ranting had taught Fargo two things. First, Lyndon was no badman. Cutthroats didn't introduce themselves before they killed someone; they walked right up and shot their victims to ribbons. Second, the man wasn't a Westerner. He had an accent typical of someone from back East, say, New York or New Jersey.

"I won't wait much longer. Then I'm coming in after you!"

Fargo was west of Lyndon now, low to the ground and almost to the grass. He had no hankering to kill the man. The question was, could he avoid it? A twitch of Lyndon's trigger finger was all it would take to blow him in half. As lawmen were fond of pointing out to drunken rowdies in saloons, buckshot meant burying.

Lyndon climbed down. Slung over his saddle horn was a pouch with a wide strap which he transferred to his right shoulder. Extra shells, was Fargo's guess. "I took you for a coward and I was right!" Lyndon yelled. "I'll bet you only kill someone when they're at your mercy. Is that how you murdered Bob and Susan? Did they see it coming? Or did you shoot them in the back?"

Fargo sank onto his stomach and twisted so he was facing Lyndon. A few more facts were apparent. The older man *was* out for revenge, not for Sanders, but for two other people who had meant a lot to him. And he wrongly believed Fargo was to blame for their deaths.

"Enough!" Lyndon roared. "I've never taken another life, but in your case I'm willing to make an exception." Thrusting the shotgun forward as if it were a lance, he stormed into the woods, tramping with head high, an ideal target if ever there was one.

Slowly rising with his knees bent, Fargo snuck to where Lyndon had been standing and began stalking the tower of righteous wrath as silently as a full-blooded Sioux. He came up on the man from the last direction Lyndon would expect; from behind.

George Lyndon had all the stealth of a bull buffalo on a rampage. "Show yourself, damn your bones! Your days of slaughter and stealing are over!"

Fargo was amazed. Did the Easterner honestly think a hardened killer, or anyone else for that matter, would step out into the open to be blasted to shreds? Eighteen feet separated them. He couldn't wait to disarm Lyndon and get to the bottom of this.

"I've been after you for months, crisscrossing the Badlands

from one end to the other. I knew that if there was any justice in the world, I'd find you."

At fifteen feet Fargo slowed to a snail's pace.

Lyndon was swinging the shotgun from side to side, so eager to shoot that his hands shook. "Sending you to hell will make me no better than you are. But it's a price I'm willing to pay so Bob and Susan can rest easier in their graves."

Fargo set each foot down gingerly, on the lookout for twigs.

"Do you have any idea how much they meant to me?" George Lyndon railed. "Robert was my only son! I loved him more than I love life, and now he's gone." Lyndon faltered, his whole body quaking. "I haven't found his body yet, but I feel it in my soul. When you cut him down, you cut out my heart!"

Twelve feet were left between them, each rife with peril. At any moment the distraught father might turn, and Fargo couldn't possibly reach him before he fired. The twelve-gauge wouldn't leave enough for even Fargo's closest friends to identify him.

Lyndon suddenly stopped, stooped, and gazed into a cluster of bushes. He stamped a foot like an angry bull, then started to pivot.

Fargo dreaded the man would turn completely around. He'd have to shoot. It was either the Easterner or him, and it wouldn't be him. Being slain for something he hadn't done was a stupid way to die. He aligned the Henry for a heart shot, his trigger finger curling. At the last possible moment, George Lyndon walked on.

"Where are you?"

Fargo had risked his neck enough. It was time to end it, and end it quickly, before Lyndon realized he was there. Reversing his grip so he held the Henry by the barrel, he took a deep breath and hurtled forward. He only had ten feet to cover. Three long strides and he would be on Lyndon like a falling tree. One blow to batter the shotgun aside, another to knock the man down, and it would be over. Just like that.

But George Lyndon wasn't the buffoon Fargo assumed. For

37

just as the Trailsman spurted toward him, Lyndon spun, his expensive English shotgun now rock steady in his hands and fixed on Fargo's abdomen.

"Die, you vermin!"

Fargo couldn't dodge. There was nowhere to seek cover. He was caught flat-footed and as good as dead.

4

For a terrible instant Skye Fargo's life teetered in the balance. He was too far from George Lyndon to hit Lyndon with the Henry. So Fargo did the next best thing. He *threw* the rifle. It was done on sheer impulse. Fargo really didn't think it would have much effect. All Lyndon had to do was sidestep and fire. But Fargo wasn't about to be blown to bits and do nothing about it. He would go down swinging. He would resist the black tide of oblivion for as long as breath remained in him.

The Henry flipped end over end, straight at Lyndon's face. Instead of sidestepping or firing, Lyndon swept up the shotgun to ward off the rifle. It struck with such force that Lyndon was jarred backward. He stumbled and nearly fell. Before he could recover his balance, Fargo was upon him.

A flying leap by Fargo bowled Lyndon over and the two men crashed to the grass. Fargo clamped his hands on the shotgun and wasn't about to let go. Lyndon, hissing, tried to bring the weapon to bear but they were too close together. And it was soon apparent his strength was no match for the Trailsman's.

Pushing the gun against Lyndon's chest, Fargo pinned him. He would still rather not hurt Lyndon if it could be avoided, but the man was making it hard. Lyndon heaved and gouged and kicked in a determined effort to dislodge Fargo and free the shotgun.

"Listen to me!" Fargo shouted. "I'm not your enemy!"

"Liar!" Lyndon raged, redoubling his attempts.

They struggled fiercely, rolling to the left, then to the right. Just when Fargo thought he had the upper hand, Lyndon rammed a knee into his ribs, and was able to free himself. Grappling for control of the shotgun, they battled like men possessed.

In George Lyndon's case, it was literally true. The man was beside himself, berserk with fury. His face was red, his eyes blazing with feral savagery, his lips drawn back to expose his teeth, just like a cornered beast. It seemed that nothing short of death would stop him.

Their next roll smashed Fargo against a tree. His left elbow bore the brunt of the blow and his arm went numb. His grip slackened.

It was the moment Lyndon had been waiting for. With a superhuman wrench, he tore the shotgun from Fargo's grasp. Crying out in triumph, Lyndon scrambled backward to gain room to use it.

"I've got you now!"

Not if Fargo could help it. He drove his right boot up and into Lyndon's crotch. A guttural grunt escaped Lyndon's lips and he sputtered like a teapot building up steam. His face changed from red to purple. The shotgun sagged.

Fargo flung himself at the man once more. Balling his right fist, he slammed it into Lyndon's jaw repeatedly. On the third blow, Lyndon's eyes fluttered and he sank onto his back. Pumping to his feet, Fargo ripped the shotgun loose and backpedaled. Both hammers were still cocked. It was a miracle neither barrel had gone off.

Fargo saw that Lyndon's hat had fallen off, revealing brown hair speckled partly white. The man's jacket was wide open, and it was plain he had no gunbelt. Wriggling his left arm to alleviate the numbness, Fargo stepped a few feet toward a log. Sitting, he rested the shotgun across his knees, pointed at the inept avenger.

In due course Lyndon twitched, mumbled, and sat bolt upright. Suddenly he froze, staring into the barrels of his own weapon. "Well, what are you waiting for? Do it, you miserable scum."

"Are you that eager to die?"

"With Bob gone, I have no reason to live. My sainted Marsha, God rest her soul, went to her reward years ago."

"Where are you from, Lyndon?" Fargo asked. He wanted to keep the man talking. The longer they did, the calmer Lyndon would become.

"Baltimore, Maryland. But what do you care? Kill me and be done with it."

Fargo had never met anyone so anxious to die. "Tell me about Bob and Susan. She was his wife, I take it?"

Lyndon bristled and started to rise, coming after Fargo despite the shotgun. Catching himself, the older man clenched his hands in impotent outrage. "Quit taunting me. You know damn well who she was! I'll be damned if you'll rub my nose in it!"

"I'd like to know what happened to them."

"As if you don't already!" Lyndon cried. Carried away by roiling emotion, he launched into a verbal tantrum. "They were on their way to the Oregon Country! Two of the nicest, most decent people who have ever lived! My Robert was going to set himself up as a lawyer, and he had high hopes of making something of himself. They signed on to join a wagon train leaving St. Joseph, but they arrived too late. Rather than wait weeks for the next wagon train to leave, they struck off on their own. Robert wrote me. He was confident they could catch up with the first train if they pushed hard. That was the second to last letter I ever received from him." Sorrow silenced Lyndon, an anguish so profound he bowed his head and tears trickled down his cheeks.

Lyndon's son had made a serious blunder. Prairie schooners weren't carriages. Robert Lyndon had no hope of overtaking the wagon train. The young couple had unwittingly put themselves at the mercy of the wilderness, a cruel mistress, indeed. To keep the elder Lyndon talking, Fargo said, "You received another letter later?"

George glumly nodded, then looked up. The fire was gone from his features. His eyes were those of a man whose spirit had been shattered by overwhelming loss. "Yes, I did. Evidently, when they were well out on the prairie, they ran into a man who told them about a new community springing up. A wonderful place to start their new lives."

Fargo's interest perked. Could it be?

"This man offered to take them there. He told them how much safer it would be than if they went all the way to Oregon. And he claimed there was plenty of good land, ripe for the taking. All they had to do was pick the site they liked." Lyndon sniffled. "Bob and Susan talked it over and agreed to go. Two days later they ran into a party of buffalo hunters. Bob slipped a letter to one of them and paid him five dollars to have it relayed to me." He slumped, as broken as a person this side of the grave. "If only Bob had turned back. He had cause, after how their guide acted."

"How's that?" Fargo said.

"In his last letter Bob mentioned how upset their guide became when they ran into the hunters. He kept telling Bob not to talk to them or join them at the fire. Bob thought it very strange. The buffalo hunters were gruff men, but friendly. They treated Susan like a princess."

As well they would, Fargo thought. Buffalo runners, as they preferred to be called, often went months without seeing a woman.

"When Robert mentioned he was thinking of giving one of them a letter to me, the guide grew upset. He warned Bob the hunters couldn't be trusted, that they might have their way with Susan, and that it was best to part company as soon as possible."

"Did your son say who this guide was?"

"Vetch. Cyrus Vetch."

A cold sensation spread throughout Fargo's chest.

George Lyndon stabbed a finger at him. "But you already know that, you conniving fiend. Because you're him! You're Vetch! And I demand to know what you did to my son and daughter-in-law!"

Fargo stood and carefully let down the twin hammers. "You're a jackass, Lyndon," he said, then shocked the man silly by tossing the shotgun to him. Lyndon caught it, his mouth agape. "If I were Vetch, you'd already be dead."

"But you have to be him!" Lyndon declared. "I saw that fellow you killed. And his horse."

"The horse broke a leg. The man tried to bushwhack me." Fargo, introducing himself, extended a hand to help Lyndon to his feet. "What we have to do is go after the real Vetch and get some answers."

Lyndon appeared dazed by the turn of events. "The real Vetch? But I was so certain—"

"We all make mistakes. Now snap out of it. There's another young couple with Vetch right this minute, and they have two daughters."

"No!" Lyndon said, aghast.

Fargo had one last question to ask. "What was the name of the community Vetch was taking your son to?" As if he didn't already know.

Lyndon reached into an inner jacket pocket and pulled out a letter. Opening it, he ran a finger down the handwritten lines. "Here it is. Paradise. Bob mentions that it's in a region where there are a lot of gypsum hills. When I came West, I asked around. All the frontiersmen I talked to told me it could only be the Badlands."

"Come on." Fargo said. There wasn't a moment to lose. He had been right to distrust Cyrus Vetch. Something was dreadfully wrong, and fear for the Webbers flooded through him. He should never have left them.

"Hold on," Lyndon said. "This is all so sudden. How do I know I can trust you? How do I know you're not in cahoots with Vetch? That you spared me just to trick me later on?"

Irritation fired Fargo's dander and he walked off. And Esther had accused *him* of having a suspicious nature! Lyndon had him beat all hollow. "Believe what you want. I don't have time to waste arguing. A little girl might be in great danger."

Lyndon hustled after him, bleating, "Not so fast, please! What's Vetch's game? How long has he been doing this? Does he work alone or is he part of a gang?"

"I don't rightly know yet," Fargo answered. He recalled the silverware and money Hiram Sanders had been carrying, and his fear for the Webbers grew. "You can ask Vetch himself." Grasping at straws, he said, "What if we have it all wrong? What if your son sent word to you that he had reached Paradise but the letter never reached you?"

"Not hardly. It's been a full year since they disappeared. Robert would have written me once a month, if not more. I'd have heard something by now."

Fargo retrieved the Ovaro and hastened toward Lyndon's horse. "I'll tell you all I know as we go. But if you're right, then I've been played for the biggest fool who ever lived. And the son of a bitch responsible is going to pay."

Something in Fargo's voice caused George Lyndon to say, "You must care quite a lot about that family you mentioned."

"They're fine folks," Fargo said, and let it go at that.

Side by side, they trotted eastward under the scorching sun. Fargo shared what little he knew about Vetch and Paradise.

"This is awful. Just awful. That monster must prey on innocent travelers all the time. I doubt Robert and Susan were the first. You'd think someone would have caught on by now and brought him to justice."

Fargo begged to differ. The scheme was too devious, almost foolproof. There was no law in the Badlands; it was wide open territory where a man's strong arm and fast gun were all that kept him alive. Vetch knew that. It was why he lured unwary pilgrims there. And the beauty of his vile operation was that the relatives of those who vanished would assume Indians or a natural disaster were to blame. There was nothing to link Vetch with the disappearances. Or there hadn't been, until Robert Lyndon snuck out that letter to his father.

Both the stallion and the sorrel were flagging by day's end. Fargo resisted an urge to push on long into the night. Riding their animals into the ground would slow them down even more the next day. So he reluctantly called a halt as twilight blanketed the glassy hills, making camp in a dry wash where they were sheltered from the wind and prying eyes.

The rabbit had started to stiffen but the meat wasn't spoiled, and soon Fargo had stew boiling. Its aroma mixed with the fragrant scent of brewing coffee, making his stomach growl. George Lyndon sat cross-legged across the fire, the English shotgun in his lap, as morose a soul as ever lived. To take the man's mind off his son, Fargo said, "You must be as hungry as I am."

"How can you eat at a time like this? I've hardly been able to touch food for longer than I care to remember."

"We have to keep our strength up."

"To be honest, Mr. Fargo, I don't much care if I live or die. My wife and my son are both gone. I have no one to live for except myself, and I'm tired of the heartache. I'd much rather join my loved ones in the Hereafter."

"And let Vetch get away with what he's done?"

"What do you think has kept me alive this long? I won't drop dead until he does. If it's the last thing I ever do, I'll make that man answer for his crimes." Lyndon fidgeted, appearing embarrassed. "Before I forget, there's something I've been meaning to say to you. I'm sorry for what I did, for jumping to the wrong conclusion. For trying to kill you. I hope you can forgive me."

"There's nothing to forgive. I might have done the same in your boots."

Lyndon shook his head. "No, I doubt that. I doubt that very much. You're not the kind to fly off the handle. Have you ever lost control once in your whole life?"

Fargo had to think on it.

"See?" Lyndon managed a wan grin. "If it's that hard for you to remember an occasion, then you haven't." He exhaled loudly. "I envy you. I've always wanted to be master of my own destiny, but I've never had what it takes."

Not quite sure he understood what the heartsick man was referring to, Fargo changed the subject. "There's something I've been meaning to say, too. From here on out, you do as I say. No matter what."

Lyndon didn't like it. "Now see here. What gives you the

right to boss me around? I have as much stake in this as you do."

"Maybe more," Fargo allowed. "But I don't want you cutting loose with that cannon of yours the second we see Vetch."

"You want me to spare him?"

"Hell, no. If what we suspect is true, I'll gladly step back and watch you blow him apart. But there may be others involved. There may be more to this than we figure. And until we've learned all there is to know, you can't go off half-cocked."

Lyndon chuckled. "Like I did when I went after you?"

"Just so we agree," Fargo said, and filled cups with coffee for each of them. After the grueling day he had been through, it was a treat to sit back against his saddle and relax, listening to the yips of distant coyotes and the hooting of a nearby owl.

"You like it out here, don't you? In the wilds?"

"I could never live anywhere else."

The Marylander took a sip. "Not me. The outdoors scare me silly, and I'm not ashamed to admit it. I was born and bred in Baltimore. My whole life was spent in the city. The only wild animals I ever saw were stray cats and dogs."

Lyndon was so green, he was lucky to have survived as long as he had while searching for Vetch. Fargo dipped his spoon into the stew to test how it tasted. "The wilderness grows on you."

"If I lived to be a hundred, I would never feel as at home as you do. I prefer a soft mattress to the hard ground. I want my food served on china instead of in tin plates and cups."

"Your son felt the same?"

"Robert? Oh, no." For the first time since they met, George Lyndon smiled warmly. "He was much more open-minded than I am. He wasn't afraid to try new things. To go West and help civilize this brave new land." George then lapsed into silence, and didn't speak even when Fargo handed him some stew.

After eating, Fargo walked to the top of the wash for a look-see before turning in. A crescent moon dominated the sky, casting the Badlands in a pale glow. The hills resembled ghostly heads rising up out of a spectral sea. To the south, a cougar screeched like a disembodied soul. Fargo relished the scene, the serenity. Moments like these were why he would never live in a city or town.

Lyndon was asleep when Fargo came back down. His stew had barely been touched but Lyndon had finished his coffee. Fargo cleaned up and turned in, relying on the Ovaro to wake him if anyone or anything tried to sneak up on them. He was so tired that falling asleep shouldn't have posed a problem, but he lay there for the longest time thinking about the Webbers, about Mary Beth and Claire. He told himself they would be fine. They *had* to be fine. Tomorrow would tell, was his last thought before drifting off.

The twittering of a sparrow brought Fargo out from under his blanket shortly before dawn. He reheated the coffee for Lyndon's benefit more than his, and munched on cold pieces of boiled rabbit as the eastern sky burst with brilliant shafts of sunlight.

They were on the go before the sun rose. Their horses were refreshed and chomping at the bit, and Fargo held the animals to a trot for as long as the morning coolness lasted. He counted on reaching the valley where he had last seen the Webbers by noon, but it was closer to one o'clock when they came within sight of the cottonwoods.

George Lyndon had been uncommonly quiet all morning. Now he sat straighter and rested the stock of his shotgun on his right thigh. "My search is almost over," he said. "And I have you to thank."

"Remember what I told you."

"Don't fret. I won't unload this buckshot into Vetch until you give me the word."

Fargo shucked the Henry and looped to the right, threading through the growth to the clearing. The Conestoga was gone. He got off the stallion and spent ten minutes reading the sign. Based on the tracks he found, the family had been fine when they pulled out early that morning with the cow tied to the gate, as before. Cyrus Vetch had ridden beside the team.

"They're alive," Fargo said.

47

"Or they were," Lyndon amended.

Fargo mounted and hurried on. The Webbers had a five-to-six-hour lead, but the Conestoga was a lumbering sloth. Fargo figured to catch up to them by five o'clock at the latest. From then on, he wouldn't leave their side until they were safely back on the Oregon Trail.

An hour out from the valley, as they were crossing a rutted plain, a round object lying among the high weeds piqued Fargo's interest. He detoured to see what it was; a busted wheel, discarded months ago, now overrun with ants.

"That could be from Robert's wagon," Lyndon said.

Or someone else's, Fargo thought as he reined to the southwest and picked up the pace. A little further on they saw a rusted stove. Further yet, a butter churn had been left to decay amid broken dishes. Edward Webber was bound to have seen them. Hadn't it made him the least bit suspicious? Fargo mused. Or did Vetch have a logical explanation?

More hills had to be traversed, more belongings had been scattered at random. "It's as if someone were leaving a trail for us to follow," Lyndon remarked.

Fargo saw it another way. All the things they had seen were ordinary household articles of little or no value. There were no gold-plated watches, no sterling silverware, no large jars of coins. They continued on.

"How can anyone commit murder?" George Lyndon unexpectedly asked. "How can one human being kill another?"

"It happens all the time," Fargo answered. "You yourself are fixing to kill Vetch, aren't you?"

"That's different. I'm seeking retribution for my son. But before this, I'd never so much as harmed a bumblebee. To even think of putting a slug into another person went against everything I'd ever been taught, against everything I am."

"To some men, squeezing the trigger is no harder than riffling a deck of cards."

"That's so cold. So brutal. You've killed a few times before, I take it?"

"A few."

"*How*? How can you snuff out the life of another person? Doesn't it eat at you afterward? Doesn't it make you so sick you need to retch?"

Fargo faced him. "I don't give it much thought. For one thing, I've never killed anyone who wasn't trying to kill me or someone else. For another, killing is part of life. Animals do it day in and day out."

"Again, that's not the same. They do it just to eat."

"Hogwash." Greenhorns had spouted such nonsense to Fargo before. "Some animals kill just for the sake of killing. Cougars will slaughter twenty to thirty sheep in a night. Grizzlies will kill other bears they find in their territory. Wolverines will butcher whatever they can catch and half the time not eat it at all. Even ants make war on each other." Fargo spied a break in the terrain, another valley or a ravine perhaps. "Animals are no different than we are."

"What a depressing notion. If that were true, why do we even bother to better ourselves? Why don't we all live in holes in the ground and only come out to bash in each other's brains when the whim strikes us?"

"That would be downright stupid." Fargo stifled a laugh. What was it about city dwellers that they came up with such silly ideas? A friend of his known as Three-Fingered Jack, a scout with the Fifth Cavalry, said it was the air they breathed. All that wood smoke and soot got into their lungs and addled their minds. Fargo just figured it was because too few had been taught to use their common sense. A little sense went a long way, as Major Augustus Powell liked to say.

The break widened, acquiring the dimensions of a large canyon Fargo had not known existed. Lush forest covered the canyon floor from end to end, an oasis in the middle of the wasteland. Wagon wheel ruts led down into the trees.

George Lyndon was in awe. "Robert wrote me that Vetch claimed there were places like this. Could Paradise actually exist?"

"If cows can fly," Fargo muttered. The road, if such it could be called, meandered lower in a series of gradual switchbacks.

The canyon walls were no more than two hundred feet high but the road covered twice that distance before it reached the oaks.

"Do you smell that?" Lyndon asked.

Fargo had caught the scent of smoke before they left the rim. The Webbers had pitched camp early again. Soon he would be reunited with them, and Cyrus Vetch would have a lot of explaining to do. The metallic click of a gun hammer brought him up short. Lyndon was fondling the shotgun as if it were a lover. "You gave me your word," he said.

"And I'll stick by it. I just want to be ready."

"Take the shells out."

The older man was annoyed and it showed. "You don't trust me all of a sudden?"

Where Cyrus Vetch was concerned, Fargo never had. Lyndon was like a pistol with a hair trigger, set to go off the second he ran into Vetch. "No, I don't. And we both know why. So do as I told you."

"What if it had been your son?" Lyndon challenged. When Fargo didn't take the bait, he testily broke the shotgun open and emptied both barrels. "There," Lyndon grated. "Satisfied?" Snapping the breech closed, he added the shells to those in his pouch.

"Keep them there," Fargo said, and kneed the Ovaro. The odor of burning wood became stronger. Off through the trees he saw a campfire. In a wide clearing sat the Conestoga. The oxen and the cow were grazing close by. Of the Webbers, there was no sign. Fargo took it for granted that Esther and the girls were in the wagon and Edward was off gathering more firewood or whatever. Vetch was probably with Ed.

Fargo rode into the clearing, calling out, "Anyone home?" In his haste to verify the family was all right he forgot one of the most important lessons a frontiersman ever learned. *Never, ever take anything for granted.* His glaring mistake was borne home the next moment when two grungy hard cases with leveled rifles came around the rear of the wagon. They fanned out, covering Fargo and the Easterner. Seconds later, from out of the woods to the east, stepped two more.

"Well, well," a stocky gunman said. "What do we have here, boys?"

George Lyndon summed up the situation nicely. "I think we're in trouble."

5

Skye Fargo was not about to reach for his Colt with four rifles trained in his direction. He would be shot full of holes before he cleared leather. So he did what he often did when he was in a poker game and he had a rotten hand, but he still thought he could come out on top; he bluffed. Leaning on the saddle horn, Fargo smiled and said, "Is this any way to greet a couple of tired strangers? All we wanted was some coffee."

George Lyndon, thankfully, caught on right away. "We saw your fire and thought you might have some to spare."

A human broomstick near the wagon glanced at the stocky gunman who had emerged from the woods. "What do you think, Pearson? What should we do?"

The man named Pearson had a swagger and a jagged scar on his left cheek. He had the air of someone with a nasty disposition, someone just itching to throw his weight around. "I don't know yet, Hicks." To Fargo and Lyndon he said, "Start talking. Who the hell are you and what the hell are you doing here?"

Fargo took a gamble. To give in too easily would make the hard cases wonder. "That's none of your business." On the frontier, a man's affairs were his own. No one else had any right to meddle.

"I'm making it my business," Pearson said, hiking his Spencer a few inches. "And if I were you, I wouldn't rile me."

Lyndon extended his arms, palms out. "There's no need for violence, young man. We're on our way to Texas. If we're not welcome here, we'll just leave."

Pearson stared at the Easterner as if Lyndon were a slug he

52

wanted to crush underfoot. "You'll go when I say you can and not before. Where are you from, old man? It sure ain't from around these parts, the way you talk and dress."

"I'm from Maryland."

"Where's that?"

"On the Eastern Seaboard."

"What do planks have to do with anything?"

Lyndon started to laugh, but when Pearson glared, he quickly turned serious. "Ever hear of the state of New York?"

"Who hasn't? That's where folks drink a lot of tea and walk around with umbrellas and parasols because they're afraid to get wet. What about it?"

"Maryland is south of New York."

"You don't say? So, what's a greenhorn like you doing so far from home without his umbrella?" Pearson snickered at his joke.

Fargo was afraid the heartsick father would say more than he should, so he spoke up. "We told you. We're on our way to Texas. And that's all you need to know."

Pearson took a step, holding his rifle as if about to swing it. "You still don't get it, do you, big man? I'm top dog here, not you. You'll do exactly as I say or you'll never get any closer to Texas than you are right now."

"Is that a threat?"

The stocky gunman motioned at Hicks. "If this contrary cur sasses me once more, blow out his wick."

All this time, Fargo had been casting secret glances around the clearing, seeking some sign of the Webbers. That there were no bloodstains was encouraging. They might be in the Conestoga, bound and gagged. To find out, he had to convince Scar Face to let them stick around. Pretending to be cowed by the threat of being filled with lead, he said, "Now hold on. My name is Lassiter. My friend's handle is Jones. We got into some trouble up in Kansas and things got a little too hot for us."

"The law is after you?" Pearson responded. "Hell, why didn't you say so in the first place? I'd as soon bust a lawman's skull as spit."

"Then we have something in common," Fargo lied. "So how about some of that coffee you've got brewing? I'll answer all the questions you have, but I'd sure like to get down. I've been in this saddle since before sunup."

"I reckon it won't hurt," Pearson said begrudgingly.

Another hard case, a black-haired man in a black vest and hat, wasn't convinced. "Hold on. Didn't the boss say something about an hombre in buckskins?"

Fargo tensed. Their leader could only be one person: Cyrus Vetch. Vetch, who wanted him dead. Vetch, who had sicced Hiram Sanders on him not once, but three times.

Pearson was studying Fargo with renewed interest. "That he did, Baxter. But buckskins are as common as freckles. Half the boys in our own outfit wear 'em. And the hombre the boss mentioned was alone, heading west. Not toward Texas. Besides, Hiram went after him. Ten bucks says he's worm food by now."

"What do we do with these two, then?" asked the fourth cutthroat.

Pearson moved to the left of the stallion and the sorrel, where he had a clear shot if need be. "Climb on down, gents, and help yourself to some Arbuckle's."

Fargo began to slide his leg up.

"But first hand over your hardware," Pearson said. "Just as a precaution, you understand. When you're ready to leave, we'll give your six-shooters back."

Since no self-respecting frontiersman would ever let himself be disarmed, Fargo was obliged to say, "No one takes my pistol."

"It's either your Colt or your life," Pearson bluntly responded. By his expression, he was hoping Fargo would choose wrongly.

The other three were cut from the same coarse cloth. Cyrus Vetch, Fargo reflected, was a treacherous serpent who surrounded himself with sidewinders. And wherever a nest of rattlers proved a threat to life and limb, there was only one thing to do. Wipe the nest out. But for now, Fargo had to play along.

54

Carefully plucking the Colt with two fingers, Fargo handed it over to Baxter. Hicks took Lyndon's shotgun.

"That's better," Pearson said. "Now we'll all get along just fine."

Fargo knew better but he climbed down and led the Ovaro to the wagon. Past it, hidden until now, were the horses belonging to the hard cases. As George Lyndon came up beside him, Fargo whispered, "Follow my lead. Be ready."

"Understood."

When they turned, Pearson and Baxter were by the fire, arguing. Fargo found the exchange of great interest.

"—shouldn't give up while there's light left," Baxter was saying. "The boss said we can't leave until we find her."

"You think I've forgotten?"

Which of the three Webbers were they talking about? Fargo wondered. Esther, Mary Beth, or Claire? Seeming as if he had no interest in what the gunmen were saying, he ambled to the fire and hunkered.

"We should keep looking," Baxter declared. "Use torches if we have to. The boss thinks she'll fetch one of the highest prices yet. Quimico has a weakness for her kind."

At the mention of the name, Fargo nearly gave himself away by looking up in alarm. Quimico was the scourge of north Texas, a renegade who delighted in torture and wholesale slaughter. Part Comanche, part white, with a dash of Mexican thrown in, he spoke all three languages fluently and had been raiding white ranches and haciendas south of the border for over a decade. The unfortunates he had butchered numbered in the hundreds. Men, he killed outright. Women, pretty women, he raped, then tortured to death. Rumor had it he liked to prolong their misery, that he reveled in it. The Texas Rangers had put him at the top of their Most Wanted list.

"I'm partial to them my own self," Pearson said.

Hicks stepped forward. "Don't even think it, Ike. The boss will have you staked out and skinned alive. Remember Grissom? After he trifled with that Mex girl the boss was fixing to sell to General Diaz?"

55

Another name Fargo had heard before. Diaz was a ranking officer in the Mexican Army who ruled Sonora as if it were his own private kingdom. In his own way, Diaz was almost as brutal as Quimico. He hated Indians and whites with equal fervor. Saloon gossip had it that the only thing he liked more than admiring his reflection in a mirror was admiring naked women. Suddenly Fargo had a whole new insight into what Cyrus Vetch was up to, and cold fury boiled up within him.

"I haven't forgotten a thing," Pearson snapped. "The boss left me in charge until Sanders shows up, so you'll do as I say, damn it."

"Sure we will," Hicks said. "Don't get your dander up."

"We know not to make you mad," Baxter added. "The last fool who did is pushing up clover."

Pearson nodded. "Just so you understand how things are." He surveyed the forest. "The blonde can't have gone far. She'll stick close, maybe try to steal one of our horses. Well, I say we help her."

Blonde? Fargo thought. That could only be Mary Beth.

"Are you loco?" Hicks asked. "If she gets away, the boss will have a fit."

Clucking like an irate hen, Pearson grumbled, "Idiots. I have idiots to work with." His voice sank so only those near the fire could hear. "I didn't say we would *let* her escape. I only said we'd *help* her try. Baxter, you go tether the horses on the east side of the clearing close to the woods. As bait. Later, when it gets dark, sneak on over and hobble them. With any luck, she won't see you."

"Oh, I get it now!" Hicks declared.

"Good. Because after Baxter hobbles the horses, I want you to climb a tree and keep watch. Pick a tree with a lot of leaves so the filly doesn't spot you. And then don't budge, not even to scratch your ass. Savvy?"

"We savvy, Ike," Baxter said.

The fourth gunman was by the wagon polishing his rifle, but Fargo wasn't fooled. The cutthroat was keeping an eye on him and Lyndon.

George had come to the same conclusion. "They have us over a barrel," he quietly complained.

"They only think they do." Fargo couldn't go into detail because just then Ike Pearson squatted to pour himself a cup of coffee.

"So, you two have taken a notion to become Texicans?" Pearson glanced at Lyndon. "Texas is no place for amateurs. To stay alive, a man has to be as good with a gun as he is with his fists. Reckon you qualify, city feller?"

"I can hold my own, thank you very much."

"Is that so? Or are you just braying to hear yourself make noise?" Pearson grinned. "Something tells me you know as much about six-shooters as a frog does about bedsheets. If I got the urge, I could pound you into the dirt without half trying."

"Could you pound me?" Fargo interrupted. "Because you'll have to if you touch him. He's my partner, and he'll do to ride the river with." Which was about as high a compliment as one man could pay another. "Don't let his looks fool you. He's as sharp as a briar and has more sand than most."

"Hmmmph," was the stocky gunman's reply.

Baxter and Hicks were leading the four mounts past the oxen and the cow. They had their backs to the fire. The gunman at the wagon was treating himself to a ladle full of water from a barrel attached to the side. And Ike Pearson had his nose buried in a tin cup.

Fargo's right hand slipped down his leg to the top of his boot. When Pearson looked away to check on the others, Fargo slipped the Arkansas toothpick from its ankle sheath and slid it up his sleeve.

"Did I hear correctly?" Lyndon asked Scar Face. "Are you and your men hunting for a blond woman? Who is she?"

"Big ears lead to big bullets," Pearson warned.

"I was only going to offer our help," Lyndon said. "Six searchers are better than four. Together, we could scour the whole area in no time."

Pearson was like a bear with a thorn in its paw. "Now why would *you* care to help *us*? I'm always suspicious of people

57

who are too damned nice. Makes me think they're hiding something."

Fargo came to Lyndon's rescue. "It's been a while since we saw a female. When a man goes without, he gets hungry for the sight of one."

"Ain't that the truth," Pearson said with false friendliness. "That's why I'm glad our boss lets us have the ones no one else will want. They might not win any prizes at a social but they keep a man warm on a chilly night."

"Any chance your boss is looking to hire some new men?" Fargo asked.

"Why? Think you'd be interested?" Pearson rejoined. "It might not be to your liking. The hours are long and the pay isn't always regular."

"So?" Fargo retorted. "We're not afraid of hard work. And any pay is better than no pay at all."

"I suppose. Tell you what, Lassiter. Come with us when we leave and you can ask the boss yourself. If he says no, no harm done."

"We'd be in your debt." Fargo fed the rooster's pride.

Presently, Hicks and Baxter returned and the hard cases made small talk, little of which was of interest to Fargo. Shortly after the sun relinquished the heavens to the stars, Baxter snuck off to hobble the horses. In the dark Mary Beth wouldn't notice. Even if she did, undoing the hobbles would take time and cause the horses to act up. The gunmen were bound to notice, just as Pearson was counting on.

Hicks had a nose as long as a rake. He kept asking questions: What kind of trouble had Fargo been in? Where had Fargo and Lyndon been to before Kansas? Did Fargo know the Bascombe brothers? Had Fargo ever been to Denver? Hicks was sure he had seen Fargo there, but using a different name than Lassiter.

Fargo made up more stories than a kid who had skipped a week of school.

Done with the hobbling, Baxter came back a second time. Hicks asked Pearson if he should go climb a tree, but Pearson advised him to wait a bit. "Too much commotion will make her skittish. Sit tight for ten minutes or so."

It was half that amount of time when the moment Fargo had been waiting for came. He'd shifted just enough so he could watch the tethered horses without anyone catching on, and when a shadow detached itself from the benighted wall of vegetation and slunk toward them, Fargo rose and stretched.

"Where do you think you're going?" Pearson asked.

"I'm tired of sitting," Fargo answered, pivoting so his right arm was within striking distance. "Thought I'd stretch my legs."

"Not now," Pearson said. "Didn't you hear me? The gal we're after might be spying on us, and I don't want to scare her off."

"Whatever you want," Fargo said. Then he looked at the horses and raised his right hand to his chin as if in surprise. "Say! Isn't that her now?"

The hard cases leaped erect. Baxter and Hick sprang to Pearson's side. The fourth man, the one by the wagon, had also straightened, and foolishly hollered, "I see her, Ike! Let's catch her before she steals a horse!"

The shadow was up and flying toward the woods before the shout died.

"You damned fool, Jeffers!" Pearson railed. "After her, boys!"

As one, the four cutthroats started forward. As they did, Fargo darted in close to Baxter, who had the Colt wedged under his belt, and sank the Arkansas toothpick to the hilt between the gunman's ribs. Baxter grunted once and folded like an accordion.

Fargo's hand closed on the Colt, smoothly whipping it free. "That's far enough, boys," he said. "Drop your irons and no one has to die."

The three men stopped and glanced back. "Baxter!" Jeffers exclaimed, and whirled, unlimbering his Smith & Wesson. His speed was middling. On his best day he couldn't hope to match Fargo, even if Fargo wasn't already holding the Colt. The blast

59

punched Jeffers backward, his arms flapping like the wings of a headless chicken.

Pearson and Hicks were riveted in their boots, but only momentarily. Swearing, Hicks made a play for his six-gun. The cylinder wasn't clear of the holster when Fargo's Colt banged and Hicks became the third hard case to kiss the earth.

That left Ike Pearson. The man in charge. The one so fond of threats and bluster. The one who acted so tough. He was the only one of the four to have a rifle in his hands, yet he'd made no attempt to use it. Pearson gawked as if mesmerized by the smoke that rose from the end of the Colt.

"Your turn," Fargo said.

Pearson's throat bobbed. "I have no quarrel with you."

"You work for Cyrus Vetch—"

"I never said Vetch was my boss," Pearson said, and threw the Spencer down. "There. See? Let me ride out and there'll be no hard feelings. What do you say?"

The twin clicks of twin hammers swung them both toward George Lyndon, who had reclaimed his English shotgun, loaded it, and had it fixed squarely on Pearson's midsection. "Are you the one?" he demanded.

Mightily striving not to show how scared he was, Pearson said, "The one what, you old goat?"

"The one who murdered my son and his wife, Robert and Susan Lyndon. They came west about a year ago."

"Never heard of them," Pearson said, backing away a step.

Lyndon placed his finger on a trigger. "Not another inch. Or so help me God, I'll splatter you all over this clearing."

"Don't," Pearson said.

"Yeah, don't," Fargo chimed in. They needed information. They needed answers. He said as much, but Lyndon ignored him.

"They were fine, upstanding young people," the Easterner said. "My Robert never harmed a soul. Susan liked to read and she never forgot a word. She would recite for us by the hour, from memory, the most beautiful of passages." As always when Lyndon dwelled on the pair, tears dampened his face.

It was then that Ike Pearson made his mistake. "You call a bunch of stupid poems beautiful? She drove us crazy mumbling that stuff. She never stopped. Juan had to slap her just to shut her up." Fear had made Pearson careless. He had shot off his mouth when he shouldn't have. And now the grim specter of vengeance incarnate advanced. "No!" Pearson cried. "Please don't!"

Fargo started to move between them but instinct warned him that if he did, it wouldn't stop Lyndon from firing. Still, he had to do something. "Lower the shotgun, George. We need him alive."

"No. You heard him. They hit Susan before they killed her." The intensity of Lyndon's emotions made him quiver as if it were the dead of winter. "I'll bet they tormented my Robert, too. For that, this worthless slime must pay."

Pearson had tears in his own eyes but not tears of sorrow. "Wait! Wait! Hear me out! It's not what you think!"

Fargo considered tackling Lyndon and wrestling the gun away for all of five seconds. While they were grappling, Pearson might gun them down. "George, listen to me. He can tell us where to find their leader. The man responsible for your son's death. Isn't that what you want more than anything?"

Lyndon's next comment was barely audible. "God help me. I can't stop myself. I truly can't."

Panic animated Pearson as he flung his arms out to ward off doom. "You don't want to kill me, old man! I can help you! I know things! I know where to find her."

It was as if Lyndon's ears were plugged with wax. He didn't hear. "Rubbed them both out as if they were bugs. The two people who meant more to me than my own life."

"I'm telling you the woman is alive!" Ike Pearson screeched.

Fargo lunged at the shotgun. He had to keep George from doing something they would both keenly regret.

But as Fargo took his first step, Lyndon's spine stiffened and his features became a mask of pure hatred. Hatred so potent, so overpowering, Lyndon was helpless in its grip, like a twig in the grasp of a tornado. The tempest raging within him was too much for any person to contain. He cut loose with both barrels at point-blank range.

Ike Pearson was propelled like so much tumbleweed a good fifteen feet from where he stood. Gore, flesh, bone, and scarlet showered the grass. What was left of him—and there was precious little from the waist up—landed in a miserable oozing heap. Though pulp and gristle from the waist up, his legs, incredibly, were intact. Amazingly, his head had also been spared, and his face betrayed astonishment at this untimely passing. The mouth that could have revealed so many important secrets was now spread wide for flies to roost in.

"Damn," Fargo said.

Lyndon shuffled in a trance to where the crumpled remains lay. "That was for Bob and Susan," he said. "This is for me." Mechanically, he pulled the hammers back again, then squeezed both triggers. The hollow *click-click* of the empty chambers was lost on him. Lyndon yanked on the hammers a third time.

"Enough!" Fargo ripped the shotgun from him. "He's dead, George. You've killed the one man who could help us."

The truth had not yet sunk in. "What?" Lyndon said dully.

"Didn't you hear him? Your daughter-in-law is still alive. And now we have no way of learning where she is." Fargo came close to smashing the shotgun on the ground. Exasperated, he simply dropped it. "I'm going after Mary Beth Webber. Stay here. Fire a shot if anyone comes."

"What?"

Fargo had squandered too many precious seconds to explain a second time. He ran toward the horses but Mary Beth had fled into the woods. "Mary!" he hollered. When she didn't reply he raced into the undergrowth. She couldn't have gone more than a few hundred feet, he figured. He would take her to the fire and quiz her about her parents and her sister. At dawn they would go after Cyrus Vetch. Or whoever was the gang's leader.

"Mary? Answer me!"

Rustling in a thicket was the only sound, but it was enough. Fargo plowed into the brush, barreling through to the other side. He was rewarded with a glimpse of a fleeing shape and gave immediate chase. The glint of golden hair in the pale starlight confirmed who it was. He couldn't understand why she was running from him unless in her overwrought state she hadn't recognized his voice. He tried again.

"Mary Webber! It's Skye Fargo! Hold up!"

She did no such thing. If anything, she ran faster.

While in midstride, Fargo remembered he hadn't reloaded after the gunfight. But he couldn't stop to do it now or the woman would elude him.

"Mary! Wait!"

Inexplicably, the figure melted into the darkness and was gone. Fargo drew up short. She had gone to ground, no doubt. Crouching, he waited for her nerves to fray. She wouldn't lie there long, not in the state she was in, and when she moved, he had her.

To the west, in the clearing, George Lyndon yelled, "Skye? Are you okay? What's going on? Did you catch her yet?"

The man could be a burr in the ass sometimes, Fargo mused. He twisted, and for a second couldn't credit his eyes. Somehow Mary Beth had gotten behind him. She held a thick branch over her head ready to bash in his skull. "Mary!" he blurted, but it did no good. Screeching like a wildcat, she swung.

6

The second of surprise that rooted Skye Fargo in place was costly. Mary Beth Webber struck him, throwing all of her weight into the blow. Fargo swept up his left arm to ward it off and winced as excruciating pain lanced clear up to his neck. Before she could strike again, he hurled himself to the right out of harm's way.

Or so Fargo assumed. But as he rose, Mary was on him, the club sweeping at his face, his shoulders, his chest. By scrabbling aside and backpedaling he avoided the worst of her onslaught, but he couldn't do so forever. He had to disarm her before she inflicted serious injury.

Fargo dove at her ankles to bring her down, only to be smashed in the shoulder and knocked onto his side. Mary suddenly reared above him, the branch arcing at his head. Fargo jerked out from under it at the last instant. The club thudded next to his ear. He grabbed hold and wouldn't let go, resisting as Mary frantically pulled and tugged. She was looking right at him but seemed to be staring *through* him, her features as blank as a slate, her eyes glazed from shock.

"Mary! I'm your friend!" Fargo tried one last time to calm her. But he might as well be talking to a boulder. She kicked, aiming at his groin. He twisted and saved his manhood, but her instep caught him on the inner thigh. He must have been struck on a nerve, because his whole body exploded with pain and glittering pinpoints of light danced before his eyes.

"Beast!"

Fargo saw Mary lever her foot again. Deciding enough was

enough, he churned toward her, rolling like a runaway log. She cried out when he bowled her over. Landing next to him, the club in her left hand, Mary Beth elevated it for another blow. But Fargo had other ideas. He threw himself on top of her, pinning her and the club, his hand a vise on her left wrist.

"Horrible beast!"

Fargo thought she would buck him to the moon. His greater weight was all that prevented Mary from heaving him off. Her ample bosom strained against his chest. Her shapely thighs pushed against his. And her warm breath fanned his neck. He couldn't help but grow aroused, although when his pole twitched, he willed it not to rise.

"Beast! You murdered my pa!"

Mary Beth pummeled him with her free fist. Fargo tasted his blood on his lip, and his eyebrow stung terribly. "Enough!" he declared, gripping her arm. "I'm not your damn enemy!"

"You killed my pa!" Mary insisted, saying it over and over and over while doing all she could to catapult him off.

"I'd never hurt him."

"Liar!" Mary tossed her head back and forth, on the verge of hysterics, her cheeks slick with tears. "You killed him! Killed him! Killed him!!"

Fargo did the only thing he could think of; he hauled off and slapped her. He hit her so hard, Mary Beth slumped, nearly unconscious, a dark rivulet staining the corner of her mouth. "Sorry I had to do that," Fargo said, even though she couldn't hear him. Mary offered no resistance as he sat up and cradled her against his body, his banded arms clamping hers to her sides.

George Lyndon was being as noisy as a brigade of cavalry. "Fargo? Are you all right? Do you need me?"

"I'm fine!" Fargo replied. "I have her. Now quiet down! I'll be there shortly."

Mary stirred and opened her lovely eyes. The madness was gone from them. More tears gushed as she leaned against him and whimpered, "Oh, Skye. They murdered my father. I saw it! I saw the whole thing!"

"I'm so sorry," Fargo said, and meant it. He had only known Ed Webber a short while but he had grown to respect the man.

"What will I do?" Mary asked, but she wasn't appealing to him. She had raised her gaze to the heavens. When no answer was forthcoming, she erupted in a waterfall of unchecked weeping, misery that knew no limit, a torrent that coated her cheeks and neck and seeped under the top of her dress.

Fargo gently held her and let Mary cry herself out. She sobbed and sobbed, clinging to him tightly, her breasts rubbing against him with every rise and fall of her slender shoulders. He tried not to think about her mounds, tried not to dwell on the exquisite sensation they provoked, but he couldn't help himself. She was so warm and soft and stimulating, he'd need to be made of stone not to be affected.

How long she cried, Fargo couldn't say. At least an hour. At length, she stopped and collapsed against him, sniffling and moaning pitiably. Without thinking, Fargo began to stroke her hair to comfort her. Mary snuggled closer, her lips brushing against his lower neck. It was all he could do to keep from molding his mouth to hers. She said something but the words were so muffled he couldn't understand her. "What was that?"

Coughing to clear her throat, Mary Beth straightened. Her blond tresses were in disarray and her dress was disheveled but she was extraordinarily beautiful, there in the starlight. Unconsciously so, for she made no effort to smooth her hair or arrange her clothes. "I thanked you for coming back. Why did you?"

"Need you ask?" Fargo couldn't be positive, what with the inky shadows that engulfed them, but she appeared to blush.

"Those men," Mary Beth said, glancing toward the clearing. "Those horrible, savage awful men—"

"The four who were here are dead. How many others were there?"

Mary gnawed on her lip.

"I need to know what happened," Fargo coaxed. "I need to know exactly what I'm up against."

"They murdered my pa."

So she kept saying, and while Fargo was reluctant to have her relive the nightmare, it would benefit both of them. "Take a few deep breaths, then tell me everything. Is your mother still alive? And what about your little sister? Where's she?"

"Those fiends took them both," Mary revealed. Her whole body shook, and Fargo thought she was going to break down again. But she controlled her roiling emotions and blinked back welling teardrops.

"Do it nice and slow. Don't upset yourself any more than you have to." Fargo gently squeezed her arm. "There's no rush. We can't go after them until daylight, anyway."

Mary Beth nodded and leaned against him, her head resting on his shoulder, her face inches from his. "Everything was fine until shortly after noon. We stopped in the clearing to rest the oxen and Bessy, our cow. Claire Marie was still upset, so Ma was trying to cheer her up."

"Upset about what?"

"About your leaving. Claire really took a shine to you. She kept calling you her angel, because you saved her doll."

Fargo recollected what Ed Webber had told him, and his expression acquired a flinty cast. "It was dumb luck I found the thing."

"Ma always claimed there's no such thing as luck. That Providence guides our lives from the cradle to the grave." Mary stopped, troubled. "But if that were so, Pa would be alive right now and Ma and Claire wouldn't be in the clutches of those vile monsters."

"Go on."

She was a while continuing. "Mr. Vetch had gone off to scout the trail ahead. He'd been gone about twenty minutes when we heard riders coming. Pa went to the wagon for his rifle. We were worried it might be Indians. But it was a party of white men, mostly. Eleven, there were, with two Mexicans and a fellow who looked to be part Indian."

"What did your father do?"

"What he always does. He greeted them with open arms. He

welcomed them to our camp and invited them to share our water and food."

Fargo felt her tremble again. He continued to caress her silken hair, knowing she would go on when she was good and ready.

"They were nice, at first. All smiles. Some of them complimented me on my looks, and a few even complimented Ma. One of the Mexicans, Juan his name was, hovered over her like a hummingbird over sugar water. Ike Pearson did most of the talking. He sat down with my pa and they were drinking coffee when—" Mary stopped, her fingernails digging into his arms. "—when Pearson nodded at the man who was part Indian and said, 'Do it, Coletto.'"

"Coletto stabbed him in the back?"

"How did you know? Yes. Pa had no warning whatsoever. The Indian pulled out a long knife and plunged it deep. Pa never cried out or bled much or anything. He just slumped over and was dead." Groaning, Mary placed her forehead on Fargo's jaw. "I couldn't believe what I was seeing. Claire screamed. Ma tried to run to Pa but Juan held on to her, laughing like it was a game. Almost all of them were cackling."

"Did the ones who rode off take your father's body with them?"

"No, they dragged it into the woods. I can find it, I bet."

"Just show me where they entered the trees, in the morning." Fargo would tend to the burial himself. It would only upset her more than she already was.

Mary resumed her account. "The next thing I knew, some of them were groping me and passing me back and forth. They pawed me like I was a fallen dove, and some of them kissed me. I fought back as best I could and even slapped a few, but they only poked fun at me."

"How did you get away from them?"

"It was Ma's doing. She nearly scratched Juan's eyes out and he had to let her go. Ma got hold of his pistol, then told Claire and me to run. The men who were pushing me around moved toward her." Mary paused, then began to talk faster and faster, as if she couldn't get it out quick enough. "I didn't want to leave but Ma made me. I had started to run to my sister when Coletto grabbed her. Ma shot at him and missed, and they were on her before she could shoot again. She was yelling for me to run for my life and Claire was bawling and Pearson was laughing and some of them turned to chase me and—"

"That's enough." Fargo cradled her chin in his hand. "You did fine. It took courage to stand up to them."

"But I didn't! I ran like a coward. Why they didn't come after me right away, I'll never know. I saw them put my ma on a horse and load up some things from our wagon, then most of them rode out, taking Ma and Claire."

"We'll find them. I promise."

Mary wept some more, fingers splayed over her face. "My life will never be the same after this. I'll never be as happy. My father is dead. My mother and sister might soon be. I want to find them, Skye. Find them and go home. The West is no place for us. It's no place for anyone decent."

Fargo knew it was her heart talking, not her head. Her hatred of the brutes who had destroyed her life had tainted her outlook.

Mary Beth lowered her arms. "I didn't mean that," she said. "I didn't mean you aren't decent. You're one of the nicest, handsomest men I've ever met. I like you a lot." To demonstrate, she kissed him, hard.

Automatically rimming her lips with his tongue, Fargo kneaded her upper back, massaged her neck. When they parted she was breathing heavily, her eyelids hooded. Another time, another place, and he would enjoy becoming even more intimately acquainted. As it was, he clasped her hand and stood. "Let's go back."

Mary leaned against him the whole way, their fingers entwined. George Lyndon was waiting at the clearing's edge, and Fargo introduced them. When Mary Beth learned that Lyndon had lost his son and daughter-in-law, she hugged him and said how very sorry she was.

After stripping the bodies of weapons, Fargo enlisted Lyn-

69

don's help in hauling them into the undergrowth. As they deposited the last one, Lyndon said, "There must be a shovel in the wagon. I'll find it and we'll bury them."

"No. Coyotes and buzzards have to eat, too."

"But it wouldn't be right."

Some vengeful killer Lyndon was, Fargo reflected. "Was it right of them to stab Ed Webber? Was it right of them to take his wife and girl? Was it right of them to kidnap your daughter-in-law?"

The Easterner became as rigid as a statue. "Susan is alive?"

"Pearson claimed she is. If you hadn't made a hole in him as big as a watermelon, he might have told us where to find her."

"Susan is alive!" The news stunned Lyndon. "I don't recall hearing him tell us that. Are you absolutely sure?"

"As sure as you're standing there."

"Sweet Susan!" Lyndon exclaimed. "We must leave right this minute! We'll push on through the night and all day tomorrow, if need be. Finding her is our main priority."

"You're forgetting Esther Webber and her daughter. Tracking them down will be easier, so they come first. By tomorrow night we should have them safe. Then we'll search the Badlands from one end to the other for your daughter-in-law."

"But who knows how long that will take? We should start as soon as possible."

"We can't hunt for anyone at night," Fargo said, and assumed that was the end of it. Time would prove him wrong.

The next hour was uneventful. Fargo and Lyndon collected extra wood and stacked it high so they could keep the fire blazing all night. While Lyndon chatted with Mary Beth, Fargo saw to the horses. He hadn't fully realized how tired he was until he sat down to rest.

His day was far from done, though. Fargo prepared coffee and gave Mary some pemmican, but she was too overwrought to eat. Lyndon, nibbling on a piece, sat by himself, aloof and adrift in his own thoughts.

"You should turn in soon," Fargo suggested to the blonde.

"I couldn't sleep if I tried. I'm too worried about Ma and Claire. What will those wicked men do to them?"

"They'll be fine," Fargo said. But the truth was, Fargo feared for their welfare as much as Mary did. The cutthroats might spare Claire. In light of her age, the child was of no use to them until she was much older. Esther, though, was in for a living hell unless the outlaws made it a policy not to lay a hand on their captives until it was decided what to do with them. Esther was older than they probably liked, but she was white, and as such she'd be of interest to any number of illicit contacts.

As if Mary were privy to his thoughts, she commented, "I still can't figure out what they wanted with us. Was it just to do their cooking and whatever?" At the mention of "whatever," she blushed once more.

Fargo had guessed the truth but he wasn't about to share it just yet. It would only make Mary more miserable than she already was. Which reminded him. "There wouldn't happen to be some whiskey in your wagon, would there?"

"As a matter of fact, there is. Do you need a drink?"

No, but Mary did, if only to relax her enough so she could sleep. But Fargo nodded and walked with her to the Conestoga. The interior was a shambles, thanks to the cutthroats. They had torn through the mountain of belongings searching for valuables. Whiskey would be high on their list, so Fargo was skeptical it was still there.

"It might be," Mary Bath responded to his doubt. "Give me a boost."

She was perfectly capable of climbing up herself, but Fargo placed his hands on her hips and lifted her high enough to find footing. Either by accident or design she leaned back against him, sparking electric tingles.

"Pa didn't want Ma to know he'd brought any, so he hid it."

"How did you find out?"

"I spied on him one night," Mary admitted, rummaging through the shambles of the family's personal effects. "I never told on him or anything. Pa and I were always close. He was a good father. All he ever wanted was to give us the life he felt we deserved. A nice home, fine clothes, all of that." She paused, her features clouding.

Fargo didn't want her to burst into tears again. To take her mind off her loss, he asked, "Do you have relatives you can stay with when you get back to Illinois?"

Mary brightened. "My uncle Harold. He has a farm west of Decatur. I spent a couple of summers there when I was knee-high to a calf." Crooking her neck, she declared, "Here it is! They missed it!"

Fargo couldn't blame them. Who would have thought whiskey would be in a burlap bag labeled Seeds? Mary unfastened the cord at the top, plunged her hand inside, felt around a moment, then grinned and drew out a bottle two-thirds full. Opening it, she held the bottle to her nose and sniffed.

"It smells like horse urine."

"And tastes like it, too."

Fargo took the whiskey and upended it, relishing a long swig. The burning liquor scorched a path down his throat to his belly, its welcome warmth spreading rapidly. "Your turn."

"I don't know if I should," Mary said. "Ma wouldn't approve."

"A few swallows won't hurt."

Mary nervously accepted the bottle, then snapped it to her lips rather than raising it slowly, resulting in whiskey spilling over her chin. Sputtering, she spit out more than she swallowed, and she screwed up her face as if she had just tasted a lemon, then shook as if she were having a conniption. "Lordy, that has to be the worst stuff ever invented! How can anyone drink it?"

"After a while it grows on you," Fargo answered. He held his arms aloft to help her down and she slid into them, giggling, her body pressed close. Fargo made a mental note not to let her drink too much. She was no more used to hard liquor than she was to dealing with hard cases like Ike Pearson.

"Let me try again." Mary wrapped her cheery lips around the bottle's mouth and carefully swallowed. A fit of coughing was still the outcome, but not as severe as before. Wiping the back

72

of her hand across her mouth, she smiled proudly. "There! I didn't do so bad, did I?"

"Better than I did my first time," Fargo said. "I had to pinch my nose to get it down." He didn't mention that he had been half her age.

Mary treated herself to another gulp. Tittering, she spun on her toes in a complete circle. "Goodness gracious! This is the best I've felt in ages! No wonder Pa hid it from us."

Three measly mouthfuls and she was giddy? Fargo reached for the bottle but she skipped several feet away and sucked on it as if it were life-saving medicine. "That's enough," he cautioned. "Too much and you'll be sick."

"Like you pointed out, I'm a grown woman. I can do as a darn well please." Mary Beth gestured at the starry vault above. "It's a nice night for a walk. Care to join me?" Taking a step, she nearly tripped over her own feet.

"Easy now," Fargo said, grasping her elbow. She couldn't possibly be as tipsy as she pretended. So she must be up to something, but it couldn't be what he thought it was. They strolled around the perimeter of the clearing, Mary Beth prattling about her childhood and how wonderful it had been to be raised in Illinois.

Fargo accepted her rambling for what it really was. Some people relieved worry by talking. If it helped her, so much the better. He listened with one ear while focusing his other on the night sounds that echoed off the high canyon walls. Panthers, coyotes, and owls were in full chorus. Which was a good omen. Had there been a large encampment of whites anywhere in the canyon, the wildlife would be as quiet as a church mouse.

Mary was going on about a cousin who had been her rival for the affections of a young man. They were at the opposite end of the clearing from the wagon, well out of George Lyndon's earshot. Shrouded by cool darkness, they might as well have been the only two people alive.

"I have something important to tell you," Mary announced.

Fargo waited. They had swapped the bottle back and forth

but neither of them had downed enough to be drunk—although she still behaved as if she were.

"I'm not a virgin," Mary said, and stared at him as if the secret she had shared rated a special reply.

"Neither am I."

"I've done it twice. Once with Barney Liverspoon over in Riverton. He asked me to the county fair and we had a grand time. I ate apples dipped in molasses, and Barney won a brass ring for me by shooting ten tin ducks in a gallery."

"Why are you telling me this?"

Mary Beth saw a tree that had been struck by lightning long ago and fallen partway into the clearing. She pulled him toward it, babbling as she did. "The second time was with Lester Hudson. He and I went together for over a year and I was sure we would be married. Then I learned he had been unfaithful so I broke it off." Sitting with her back to the bole, Mary patted the ground. "Sit with me a spell. Please."

Fargo glanced at the fire. A blanket had been spread beside it. Lyndon was so anxious to head out after his daughter-in-law at first light, the man had already turned in. So the two of them could do as they pleased without being intruded on. Indulging in another swallow of rotgut, Fargo sank to the ground next to the blonde.

"You might not think it to look at me," Mary Beth said, "but I'm mature for my age. More than most, if I say so myself."

Fargo was feeling too sorry for her to come right out and say she was lying. Her upturned face, as inviting as a ripe peach, stirred him lower down. "What is all this leading up to?" he asked. As if he didn't know.

"Help me forget for a little while."

"I don't know." Fargo had never taken unfair advantage in his life. He had no need to. Women naturally found him attractive.

"What's wrong? Don't you think I'm pretty?"

"You're one of the prettiest women I've ever met," Fargo conceded. And she was, with those strawberry lips of hers and that golden mane of lustrous hair and her tantalizing figure. She would turn heads on any street and make men wish they were hers. As young as she was, she didn't realize the power she had. When she did, hordes of admirers would swarm around her like bears around a beehive, eager for a taste of honey.

Mary Beth faced him. "You're just saying that to be polite."

"No, I'm not."

"Prove it."

The gauntlet had been thrown down. Fargo had a choice. He could get up and escort her back to the fire. Or he could do what his twitching manhood was goading him to do, and take her into his arms. For a few seconds his decision hung in the balance. Then she leaned forward. Her tempting lips were close to his, her eyes shining with a hunger that matched the hunger in his loins.

"Well? Are you just going to sit there? Or will you help me forget the terror of this day, if only for a little while?"

"Since you put it that way—"

Fargo's arms went up and around her and Mary melted into them like hot wax, her mouth greedily meeting his halfway. Kissing her was bliss, and in no time Fargo had forgotten about Cyrus Vetch, forgotten about the traffickers in female flesh, and most importantly, he had forgotten about George Lyndon.

Skye Fargo knew from his own experience that a person who is starving appreciates food a hundred times more than a person who has been enjoying three meals a day. A person trekking across a parched desert appreciates water more than someone who lives by a river. And those who have gone without usually can't get enough of what they have been denied. The starving person can't get enough food. The poor soul dying of thirst can't get enough water. The same held true for everything from sweets to sex.

Mary Beth Webber was a living example. By her own admission she had not been with many men. She had gone without for a long time. Now, having the chance to end her sexual fast, the hunger that had built up inside her was released in a scalding burst of raw passion. It was a frenzy of desire so fierce, that some lovers would be ill at ease.

Not Fargo. As her lips greedily kissed every square inch of his face and neck, as her hands roamed over every part of his body, he matched her carnal abandon with his own. Her sensual craving aroused him as much, if not more, than her radiant beauty. Any man would want her. Any man would feel his manhood harden, his blood quicken, and prickling warmth spread like wildfire.

Their lips met and fused. Although inexperienced, Mary Beth had natural flair. She knew just what to do to incite him the most.

Her silken tongue entwined with his, and Fargo sucked on it as a child might suck on sugar candy. His hands explored her soft, inviting nooks and crannies, roving down over her sloping shoulders to her pillowy breasts. Even through the dress the hardness of her nipples was delightfully obvious. He pinched them and she squirmed and cooed.

"Oh, Skye, what you do to me."

The feeling was mutual. Fargo kissed her again, delving his tongue deeper, his hands venturing lower to her tight buttocks. He kneaded them, pried at them, and she wriggled as if she were seated on hot coals.

"Mmmmmm," Mary groaned.

Fargo's tongue licked a path across her cheek to her left ear. He fastened onto her earlobe, his hands traveling to her hips, which were rising and falling in small rhythmic motions as if he were already buried inside her.

"Never stop. It feels so marvelous."

She had nothing to fear, Fargo mused. He squeezed her thighs, making her hips rise higher. When his fingers probed between them, Mary began to pant loudly and bit his chin. In no rush, he left her thighs alone for the time being and devoted himself to other areas. Her hair was velvety soft to the touch, her skin marble smooth.

Mary Beth had her hands on his chest. "You're getting me all excited," she huskily commented.

Wasn't that the general idea? Fargo's mouth found a spot on her neck that caused her to arch upward. He licked and nibbled it while she ground against him as if the friction from their bodies were needed to start a fire. She was wonderfully uninhibited, giving free rein to her longings.

Fargo gasped in pleasure when her hands, out of nowhere, descended on his manhood. She rubbed him, up and down and around and around, until his self-control teetered on the brink and he had to grit his teeth in order not to explode prematurely.

"Mercy me," Mary breathed. "I had no idea."

She would, soon enough. Fargo cupped both her breasts at once and worked them as a baker would work soft dough. Kissing her, he began to undo the top of her dress to gain access to her charms. She raised her hands to help but he gently pushed them away. Her assistance wasn't needed, and he would much rather have her hands on *him*.

Idly, Fargo glanced toward the fire. The blanket and the bulge under it assured him that George Lyndon was in dreamland and wouldn't come walking up at an awkward moment. He could fully relax and enjoy himself.

"Ohhhhhh," Mary Beth exclaimed when Fargo opened her dress enough to slide a hand in. Parting her underthings, he made contact with her breast, with her nail of a nipple. Pinching it was like throwing limbs on a fire. She moaned and thrust against him, her mouth seeking to devour him alive.

Some women were more sensitive in certain parts of their bodies than other women might be. In Mary Webber's case it was her glorious globes. Her whole body trembled at the slightest pressure. When he stretched her right breast by pulling on the swollen nipple, she about lifted him off the ground. Her breath was hot enough to roast him alive, her hands fluttering everywhere as if she couldn't get enough of his muscular form.

"I want you so much!"

Fargo eased lower, feasting on the sight of her melons. They were well rounded with larger-than-usual nipples, long and thick and sweet to the taste. Her fingernails gouged deeper when he rolled one with his tongue. Sliding his hands lower, to her thighs, he stroked and petted her without once touching the center of her womanhood. He wanted to prolong her pleasure, to draw it out to the point where she couldn't take it any more.

The wind soughed through the trees, rustling the leaves. Elsewhere in the canyon a night bird twittered, and far to the east a cougar screeched. Insects buzzed noisily, crickets chirping in legion numbers.

All of which further relaxed Fargo. No enemies were after them. They were safe for the moment and could let down their guard.

No sooner did the thought cross Fargo's mind than he heard the faint scrape of a hoof on stone. Instantly he lifted his head and looked to the southwest, the direction the noise came from.

"What is it?" Mary Beth asked.

"Hush." Fargo listened for the sound to be repeated but over a minute went by and it wasn't. The crickets never stopped chirping. None of the horses, including the Ovaro, nickered or stamped. Lyndon still slept peacefully. So maybe it had only been his imagination. "It was nothing, I guess."

Mary giggled. "Then what are you waiting for? I need warming up. I'm breaking out in goose bumps."

That she was, but they faded away when Fargo lavished her breasts with more attention. Before he was through, she was heaving and gasping loud enough to be heard in San Antonio, and Fargo smothered her mouth with his own to quiet her. Mary's tongue was molten fire, dipping and gliding, stroking his own inner inferno.

Fargo felt her pluck at his gunbelt. He helped her remove it as she unfastened his pants, pulling on his buckskin shirt so she could slide her hands up under it. For his part, he hiked at her dress to gain access to her nether regions. Her thighs were as perfect as a woman's could be, and he caressed them from knee to hip and back down again, the heat between her legs rising higher and higher.

"Ohhhhhhh, Skye."

Fargo was so engrossed in her tempting treats that he lost track of where her hands were. A brazen little hussy, she surprised him by suddenly enfolding his manhood in a warm palm. It was his turn to groan and stiffen as she lightly ran her hand from top to bottom. When she cupped him, he thought that he would shoot up into the trees.

"Like that, do you?"

Her taunt inspired him to move onto his knees between her legs.

Mary Beth was puzzled. "What are you doing?"

Fargo didn't tell her. She would find out soon enough. Bending, he inhaled her earthy fragrance as his mouth settled on her moist slit.

"Oh! Oh! No! No one has ever—!"

Whatever else she was going to say was drowned out by her cry of rapture when Fargo delved his tongue into her boiling center. She wheezed like a marathon runner and gripped his head. The press of his tongue on her tiny knob sent her into a paroxysm of total abandon. Mary shoved his face up into herself, her thighs opening and closing, her whole luscious body quaking.

"More! Oh, Skye, more!"

Fargo honored her request by licking and sucking until his mouth was sore and his tongue was fit to fall off. She was groaning nonstop when he rose and returned to her mounds. Her nipples were now like iron spikes. One touch and Mary vibrated like a violin string being tuned.

His pole straining for complete release, Fargo shoved his pants down to his knees and aligned his member with her opening. Teasingly, he rubbed up and down without penetrating. Mary grabbed his hips and tried to pull him into her but he held off for another minute. Then, without warning, he rammed into her like a battering ram into a castle door. She came clean up off the ground, her arms going around him as if she were drowning and had to cling to him for dear life.

"Ahhhhhhhh!"

Fargo hoped to hell George Lyndon was a heavy sleeper. Because with each powerful thrust, Mary Beth cried out. She met his thrusts with her own, matching his tempo. Pacing himself, Fargo transported her to the edge, and over.

"Skye!" Mary exclaimed. "I'm there!"

Fargo felt her gush, felt her spurt like a geyser as her inner walls constricted. He pounded into her tunnel, again and again and again, harder and harder. Her orgasm was intense, her eyelids fluttering uncontrollably, her body thrashing wildly. He had done as she requested. He had helped her forget, for a while at least.

To relieve the weight on his knees, Fargo gripped her soft bottom and shifted, never breaking rhythm. Mary buried her face against his chest, pumping with a fervor few would believe she possessed. Both of them were lost in sexual ecstasy. Their joining lasted longer than even Fargo reckoned it would. They were caked with perspiration when his explosion came. The whole world spun, the stars danced. It was one of the best, ever.

For a while time had no meaning. There was just the two of them, overcome by delirious sensations. Mary cried out again, sounding remarkably like the cougar, a scream bound to wake anyone within ten miles. But Fargo didn't care. What they did was none of Lyndon's business.

Coasting to an exhausted stop, Fargo lay on top of Mary, cushioned snugly, at peace, content. Her fingers plied his hair, her lips nibbled his forehead. He had no hankering to get up, to even move.

"Thank you."

Fargo should be the one thanking her. He kissed her mouth, her cheeks.

"I suppose we should go back. Mr. Lyndon will think I'm a loose woman. I don't know what he'll say."

"He has no right to say anything."

"Don't get mad if he does. The poor man has been through enough. Looking into his eyes is like looking into bottomless wells of sadness. I feel so sorry for him."

So did Fargo, but Lyndon's son—and Mary's father—had partially brought their fates on themselves. Ike Pearson had been right about one thing. The wilderness, like Texas, was no place for amateurs. Greenhorns were helpless sheep just waiting to be sheared by curly wolves like Pearson and Vetch.

Cyrus Vetch. Fargo still wasn't sure about him. Pearson had denied Vetch was the leader of the outlaws. Had he been lying? Or was it really someone else, someone Fargo hadn't met yet?

Mary Beth reached up to button her dress. "I'm getting cold. Can we go back?"

The air was growing chill, a welcome relief from the blistering heat of day. Rising, Fargo dressed and strapped on the Colt. It amused him to see Lyndon hadn't budged. Mary's cries had to have awakened him. He must be feigning otherwise so as not to embarrass her when they returned.

They strolled across the clearing, Mary taking Fargo's calloused hand in hers. "Never say a word of this to my mother or

I'll never live it down. In her day women didn't do things like this. They were different. She says the only man she ever let touch her was Pa, and then only after they were married."

Fargo grinned. With all due respect to Esther Webber, he didn't believe women had been any different in her day than they were now. Ladies liked to hide the fact they lusted after men as much as men lusted after them. Many prided themselves on their morals, their scruples, and they would never admit they felt the same desires as everyone else.

"Poor Mr. Lyndon must be awfully tired," Mary commented. "He hasn't moved."

They were close enough to the fire that Fargo could see the blanket clearly. Something about the bulge under it struck him as wrong. Releasing Mary, he ran the rest of the way. "George?" There was no answer, so he gripped the lower edge and yanked the blanket off.

"Land sakes!" Mary Beth declared.

Fargo swore and kicked the bundle of clothes, and his own saddlebags, which Lyndon had placed under the blanket to trick them. Recalling the sound of a hoof on stone he had heard earlier, Fargo dashed to the animals.

The sorrel was gone.

Mary had dogged his steps. "I don't get it, Skye. Where did Mr. Lyndon go? Why did he leave?"

"Susan Lyndon."

"His daughter-in-law?"

"I shouldn't have told him she's still alive. Now he won't rest until he's found her." Fargo wanted to beat his head against a tree. Or, better yet, beat Lyndon's head against a tree. George's rashness had not only put him in deadly peril, but them, as well. If he fell into the outlaw's clutches, he might tell what had happened to Pearson and the others. The cutthroats would leave no stone unturned in their quest for revenge.

"What do we do?"

Fargo had hoped to have Lyndon watch over Mary so he could ride on alone. He would get more done, and faster, when he did not have to watch all their backs at once. Now Mary had to be spirited to safety, further delaying his hunt for her mother and sister. "At dawn we're going to find somewhere you can hide."

"You're not leaving me alone, if that's what you're thinking. Where you go, I go."

"I don't want you hurt."

Mary Beth had a stubborn streak. "It's my mother and sister we're talking about. I have a right to go. You'll need me."

As the saying went, Fargo needed her to tag along like he needed a hole in the head. He tried to think of a convincing reason but all he could come up with was, "It's for your own good."

"I'll be the judge of that. You said I'm a grown woman, remember?"

Fargo wished she would stop bringing that up.

"I make my own decisions. And my place is with you. I can look after Ma and Claire once we find them. You'll have your hands full with those killers."

Fargo sighed. To argue would be pointless. Once a woman made up her mind, changing it was like changing the course of a river. It couldn't be done. "If you tag along, you'll do as I say at all times. Is that clear?"

"Of course."

Walking toward the fire, Fargo said, "We might as well turn in. There's nothing more we can do until daylight."

"Shouldn't we go after Mr. Lyndon before it's too late? We can light torches and use them to track by."

"He already has over an hour lead on us," Fargo said. "Tracking by torchlight is slow work. We couldn't catch up with him before dawn. Even if we did, he would see us coming and light a shuck."

For someone who had just given her word to do as Fargo told her, Mary Beth had an objection to everything. "For all you know, he'll be sound asleep by then. I'm not tired. Saddle a horse for me and we're off."

"Not until morning," Fargo insisted.

"Why do I have the idea you're treating me like I'm Claire's age?" In a huff, Mary Beth rotated and flounced to the fire. She scooped up the blanket Lyndon had used, gave Fargo the sort of look that implied he was related to worms, then climbed into the Conestoga. "You stay out there. I'm not in the mood for your company."

"Females," Fargo said under his breath. Hunkering, he poured himself a cup of coffee and pondered. For two bits he would let her fend for herself and go on. Well, maybe three bits.

Nothing had gone the way it should since Fargo found that doll. Thanks to an act of kindness, he was caught up in a whirl-wind of violence and bloodshed with no way out. All because he wasn't about to desert Mary or her mother or sweet little Claire.

He stayed up until one in the morning. Finally convinced no nasty surprises were in store for them, Fargo rose and cat-footed to the Conestoga. Mary Beth was sound asleep, snoring lightly. She had brushed out her hair and cleaned herself up and was stunning, an angel in repose. Without her being aware, he reached in and stroked her brow. Mary mumbled and turned on her side, her golden locks cascading over her face.

After extinguishing the fire, Fargo carried his bedroll to the Conestoga and unfolded it underneath the wagon. He was a long time dozing off. It seemed he had hardly closed his eyes when an unusual noise snapped him out of a deep sleep. Sitting up, he drew the Colt and scanned the clearing.

Dawn was half an hour off, the brightening sky beginning to relieve the gloom. Fargo shook his head to dispel cobwebs. He neither heard nor saw anything out of the ordinary, anything to account for being jarred from dreamland.

"Moooooooooo."

The plaintive bellow of the cow brought a smile to Fargo's lips. It was the four-legged rooster that had woken him up. Slid-ing into the open, he made a circuit of the camp, just as a pre-caution. Stretching his legs got his blood pumping. He threw his saddle on the pinto, and saddled a dun that had belonged to one of the gunmen for Mary Beth. As he rekindled the fire, the Conestoga's canvas cover framed her rising figure.

"Morning, Skye." Mary stretched like a cat. "Sorry about my tantrum last night. No hard feelings, I trust?"

"None. Climb down and we'll be on our way."

"You have a forgiving disposition for a man. A lot like my pa." Frowning, Mary corrected herself. "A lot like my pa was. God rest his soul."

The mention brought Fargo to his feet. He had her point out the spot where she had seen the gunmen enter the trees with her father. Finding Ed's body took no time at all. Pearson and company had gone a dozen feet, and dropped it. Already an animal had been at the face. Ed's nose had been chewed partly off and his lower lip was entirely gone. Fargo buried the man deep so the scavengers couldn't finish what they had started.

A fiery crown of a sun heralded the new day as Fargo and Mary Beth Webber rode to the southwest. He had untied the oxen and Bessy so they could graze at will. The Conestoga was left where it was.

"I just hope no one comes along and steals it," Mary remarked.

Fargo was adjusting his bandanna. "Not very likely," he said. For although the wagon contained all the worldly goods the Webbers owned, there was little of real value. The outlaws had only taken some money and jewelry. Butter churns and rocking chairs were of no interest to them.

Ages ago a section of canyon wall had collapsed, creating an earthen ramp. The tracks led up to it and to the south. The prints of Lyndon's sorrel stood out from the rest. It had a cracked front shoe, and if Lyndon wasn't careful, he would soon find himself afoot. Which, come to think of it, Fargo mused, would be for the best. He would make George take Mary back, freeing himself of the burden of looking after her.

Mary didn't say two words the first hour. As the sun warmed the Badlands, the warmth brought her to life. Several times he caught her studying him, and he had a fair inkling why. But he let her pick the moment to spring it on him, which she did as they neared a knoll.

"Skye, can I ask you something?"

Fargo grunted.

"Why haven't you ever taken a wife? A handsome fellow like you? Any woman would be proud to have you as her husband."

"Forget it."

Mary could be as innocent as a newborn babe when she was of a mind. "Forget what? All I did was ask a question."

Fargo was not willing to let her off the hook so easily. "All you did was ask me to marry you."

Speechless with indignation, Mary Beth puffed out her cheeks like a chipmunk about to go on the warpath. "What gall! I did no such thing! My folks raised me better than that. It's not fitting for a woman to ask the man."

"It wouldn't matter if it were. My answer would still be the same. No."

Mary was fit to bean him with a rock. "You can be very rude, do you know that? After what we shared last night, I'd think you would be more considerate. What we feel for each other is special." She paused. "Why do you think I was proposing, anyhow?"

"It was at the back of your mind. You thought that by bringing up marriage, you would get me to thinking about how nice it would be being your husband. Then I'd propose. In a roundabout way, you were asking me to ask for your hand in wedlock."

"That's the most ridiculous notion I've ever heard," Mary said without conviction. She visibly wrestled with another question. "But for the sake of being silly, let's say you're right. Why did you say no?"

"I made my feelings plain the day we met," Fargo said. "There's too much of the West I haven't seen yet, too many things I haven't done, for me to set down roots." He slanted toward the knoll. From the top they would be able to see for a mile or more.

"You put a lot of stake in your freedom, don't you?"

"Without it, life isn't worth living." Fargo valued being free more than great wealth, more than power, more than all the comforts civilized life had to offer. In that respect he was a lot like the Sioux, with whom he had spent considerable time when he was a young, frisky colt. "If I can't be free, I'd rather be dead."

A new voice casually stated, "That can be arranged."

Fargo reined up and lowered his right hand toward the Colt, then froze. He was covered by the twin barrels of an English shotgun held by a man he had befriended. "Is this what it's come to, George? You'd kill me with no qualms?"

George Lyndon walked down the knoll, the shotgun rock steady. "I'm sorry. But it isn't as if I've tried to deceive you. Susan comes first. I've lost Robert, but I'll be damned if I'll lose his wife, too. I'll do whatever it takes to save her. I'll even go so far as to steal your horses so you can't follow me."

"Because your sorrel went lame," Fargo said.

Lyndon planted himself at the slope's base. "I keep forgetting how talented a tracker you are. Yes, my horse threw a shoe. I was at my wit's end, wondering what I was going to do, when I spotted you coming. Now climb on down and let me have that stallion of yours."

"Over my dead body."

"I was hoping it wouldn't come to that," Lyndon said, and pulled back a hammer. "But if you resist, you leave me no choice."

8

Skye Fargo stayed in the saddle. The Ovaro was as much a part of him as his arms and legs. He would never let anyone take the pinto, even at the cost of his life. To him, the stallion was more than a lowly beast of burden. It was his friend. He was as fond of it as most folks were of their dogs and cats. More so.

"I mean it," George Lyndon said, thumbing back the second hammer. "Climb down, or in about ten seconds there won't be enough of you left to scrape up with a spoon."

Loyalty to the Ovaro wasn't the only reason Fargo stayed put. In the past twenty-four hours he had been shot at, punched, kicked, and clawed. He had been pushed, prodded, stomped, and gouged. Others had tried to bash in his brains, carve him up like a turkey, and crush him to a pulp. He was sick and tired of it, and he wasn't going to take it anymore.

Mary Beth clasped her hands as if in prayer. "Please, Mr. Lyndon! You can't! Not after all he's done for you."

"I won't let anyone stand in the way of saving my daughter-in-law," Lyndon reiterated. "Now, enough talk. Get off the damn stallion!"

Fargo stared down into the twin barrels. The buckshot would rip him to shreds. The only consolation was that it would be a quick, relatively painless end, over so fast that he would be dead before he realized he had been hit.

"Do it!" Lyndon fumed. He sighted along the shotgun and they locked eyes.

"No!" Mary yelled.

Seconds dragged by slower than snails. Fargo had heard that

at the moment before death, many people saw their whole lives flash before them. He thought of some of the beautiful women he had known. Gretchen Davenport, who had the bluest eyes he'd ever seen. Melody Britches, as feisty as any man, in bed or out. Bethany Cole, the kind of schoolmarm every schoolboy wished they had. He recalled the last time he had been to California, standing on a sandy beach at sunset, the sky painted vivid red, orange, and yellow, the ocean almost as blue as Gretchen Davenport's eyes, the surf hissing at his feet. He remembered being in the geyser country of the central Rockies, remembered seeing the largest geyser of all erupt, spewing scalding hot water and steam hundreds of feet into the air. He had seen so much in his travels, more than ten men saw in their whole lifetimes. If this were his day to die, he could do so with no regrets. But he doubted it was.

Focusing on the Easterner, who had turned to stone, Fargo said, "If you're going to do it, get it over with."

Lyndon jerked the shotgun down. "I can't," he said forlornly. "I just can't."

"I didn't think you could."

"But I almost killed you when we first met. I would have, if you hadn't gotten the better of me." Lyndon was disgusted with himself. "And I killed Pearson without any qualms. What's happening to me? Have I gone weak-kneed all of a sudden?"

"It's not weakness," Fargo said. "There's a difference between killing someone in cold blood and killing someone who deserves it."

"There is?" Mary Beth said.

Lyndon's shoulders slumped. "I should be glad, shouldn't I? I'm not a vicious animal, like the ones who slew my Robert. There's still a shred of humanity left in me. Not that it will count for much in the Hereafter." He bobbed his chin to the south. "What are you waiting for? Leave me. I'll go on foot from here on out."

"We can't abandon you," Mary said. "It wouldn't be right."

No, they couldn't, Fargo reflected. Lyndon would succumb

to thirst or starvation long before he overtook the outlaws. "You're coming with us, George. You'll ride double, taking turns on each horse. It will slow us down but it can't be helped."

The older man was astounded. "You'd do that for me? After what I just tried to do to you?"

"Climb on the dun," Fargo directed.

"What about my sorrel? It's just over the knoll."

They had to leave it behind, Fargo decided. Its foreleg was swollen but would heal. The horse would just have to fend for itself until they came back.

On into the Badlands, they traveled at a brisk walk, which was as fast as they could go. Otherwise they risked having the dun give out on them. Fargo stopped frequently so their mounts could rest and so Lyndon could switch horses.

The terrain soon changed. They saw fewer glassy hills and more grassy ones. It was dry grass, because the whole countryside was parched. And by the middle of the afternoon, so were they. Sweat rolled off Fargo in drops. His buckskins were soaked. He barely had enough moisture in his mouth to swallow.

"I pray to God my ma and my sister are alive," Mary Beth mentioned, running a sleeve across her forehead. "I still don't see why those terrible vermin took Claire. Ma, I can understand. They'll have their way with her, won't they, Skye? They'll violate her. One of them will claim her as his own."

Fargo had held off telling Mary the truth long enough. "It's worse than that."

"What could possibly be worse?"

"Yes, what?" Lyndon interjected. "They're common riffraff, nothing more. They rob and kill. That's all, right?"

"Wrong," Fargo said.

Mary was confused. "I'm afraid you've lost me," she confessed.

George Lyndon's expression grew more haggard than ever. "Lord, no. Please don't say what I fear you're going to say."

At moments like this, Fargo sometimes felt an anger he

couldn't quite make sense of. In this instance, it wasn't directed at the outlaws so much as at life itself. It was plain wrong that innocent people like Esther and Mary and Claire had to suffer. It was plain unjust that a man who had never hurt a fly, a decent man like George Lyndon, had to endure the agony of losing a son. When Bible-thumpers told Fargo that the Almighty looked after those who believed, he had to wonder if they went through life with their eyes closed.

"What is it?" Mary asked anxiously. "What are those despicable men going to do to my mother?"

Fargo didn't mince words. "They traffic in female flesh. They sell women to buyers on both sides of the border. The prettier the woman, the higher the price she fetches. Your daughter-in-law, George, must have been sold long ago. Esther won't be auctioned off for a while yet. As for Claire, they probably aim to raise her and sell her when she's older. Or—" Fargo couldn't bring himself to finish.

"Or?" Mary Beth said. "Or what?" When he refused to elaborate, she turned as white as chalk, swayed, and had to grip the saddle horn for support. "They wouldn't! Not that! Not to a little girl!"

"Other people don't live by your standards," Fargo said. "What you think is wrong they think is fine."

"But there are limits," Mary said, her voice rising. "Lines we should never cross. Stealing, murder, rape, that's all evil. And to harm a child is the worst evil of all."

"Some men like being evil."

Mary was close to tears. "That shouldn't be."

"I agree. But how we believe things should be, and how they are, aren't always the same. All we can do is live with it, and make the best of the cards we're dealt." Fargo pulled his hat brim lower against the sun. "We're not prairie dogs. We don't have the luxury of running into a burrow whenever life isn't to our liking."

"Aptly put," Lyndon said. "But I'd go you one better. Instead of making the best of the cards we're dealt, I'd say we have a responsibility to go out and make the world a better place to live in."

A bitter laugh tinkled from Mary. "Until yesterday, I always believed the world *was* a wonderful place to live. Now I see I was wrong. It's a horrible world, filled with evil and wickedness. Why does God give us life if we're only meant to suffer?"

"If I knew the answer to that, young lady," Lyndon said, "I'd be the wisest person alive. People would flock from all over to hear me discourse on the meaning of life. But, of course, I don't have the answer. No one does."

The two of them jabbered on and on about the meaning of life, but Fargo was more interested in a column of smoke rising a couple of miles to the southwest. It wasn't wispy, as tendrils from a campfire would be. This was thick and gray, rising in coils like smoke from a chimney. The tracks they were following led straight toward it.

Fargo let the heartsick father and the grief-stricken daughter chatter on for another mile. By then they were entering a valley twice as wide as any they had come across so far. A large herd of cattle made up of several breeds grazed unattended. The smoke rose from a cluster of buildings located near some cliffs on the far side. Raising a hand, Fargo halted.

"Say, is that a fort?" George Lyndon asked. "Where the blazes did it come from?"

"Look at all those cows," Mary said. "It must be a ranch."

Fargo pointed at a crudely painted sign someone had nailed to a post imbedded beside the trail. "You're both wrong." In bold, scrawled letters was the name PARADISE. Under it someone had written, POP. 29. But the 29 had been crossed out and someone else had written 28. Then the 28 had been marked off, to be replaced by a 27.

"Then it *does* exist! Vetch wasn't lying!" Lyndon was on the dun, behind Mary, and he reached around her to grab the reins. "What are we waiting for? In half an hour we can be reunited with our loved ones."

"Rush on in there and you'll never live to see Susan," Fargo predicted. The ramshackle structures, blurred by a shimmering heat haze, gave him the same feeling of unease he'd experienced the time he had stumbled on a snake den. A winter den, it had been, crammed with hundreds of sinuous reptiles, all of them slithering and coiling and hissing in one gigantic mass, poisonous and nonpoisonous serpents alike. Looking at them had made his skin crawl. Just as looking at Paradise did.

Lyndon wasn't pleased. "What else would you have us do? Sit here twiddling our thumbs?"

"We'll twiddle later," Fargo said with a poker face. Then he spurred the stallion into a gully. It might be too late; someone in Paradise might already have spotted them. Then again, they were still a mile off, and at that distance they could well be mistaken for members of the gang. Hopping down, he climbed to the top, his spurs jangling. As he lay flat, the other two joined him.

"What's your plan?" George Lyndon asked.

"We'll wait until the sun goes down, then sneak on in."

Lyndon and Mary Beth exchanged looks. "That's it?" the Easterner demanded. "You call that a plan? Why delay so long? One of us should create a diversion, maybe by starting a fire. Those scum will be so busy putting it out, we can scour the whole town for Susan, Esther, and Claire."

"In broad daylight?" Fargo scoffed. "We'll be caught."

"Not if we're careful," Lyndon said. "Under cover of the smoke and confusion, we can move freely, right under their noses."

Fargo counted seven buildings, one of them an outhouse. Paradise was too small for the older man's ruse to work. "It's not worth the risk."

Lyndon unsheathed his verbal claws. "Who are you to say? It's not your daughter-in-law we're trying to save! It's not your mother or your sister! What the hell gives you the right to decide what we'll do?"

"I'm thinking clearly," Fargo replied.

"And we're not? Our hearts are ruling our heads? Is that what you're saying? Damn it all, man! Every minute we delay is another minute our loved ones suffer. How can you blame us?" Lyndon gripped Fargo's arm. "In God's name, we have to do *something,* and we have to do it *now!*"

"Keep your voice down," Fargo warned. Noise carried far in open spaces. And while they appeared to be all alone, at any moment members of the gang might ride into the north end of the valley.

But what bothered Fargo the most was Lyndon's demand that they act immediately. As much as Fargo hated to admit it, Lyndon had a point. Waiting for nightfall was the smart thing to do, in his estimation, but sunset was five to six hours away. Every minute increased the odds of harm coming to Esther and Claire. Against his better judgment he heard himself say, "All right. But I'm going in alone."

As was to be expected, Lyndon and Mary both objected. "Why only you?" Lyndon responded. "They're our relatives."

Mary harped on the same thing. "My mother and my sister are there. If you think I'm willing to sit here and do nothing, you're sadly mistaken."

Fargo faced them. "Either I go alone or no one does until after sunset. One person has a better chance of escaping notice than three. I'll find out where the captives are kept, and if I can get them out, I will. If there are too many guards, I'll come back and we'll all go in after dark. Agreed?"

Neither Mary nor George replied right away. Fargo could tell they didn't like it, not one little bit. Lyndon broke the tense silence first, saying, "Very well. You can blend in better than we can. But if you're not back in two hours, I'm going in, too."

"Same here," Mary said.

They were asking for trouble, but arguing would be a waste of Fargo's breath. The pair would do as they wanted, and hang the consequences. "It's your lives," was his only comment as he slid down the slope and walked to the sorrel.

Lyndon was surprised. "You're taking that horse instead of your own?"

Yes, Fargo was. Ovaros were rare, and any man who rode one tended to draw attention to himself. If lookouts were posted, they would know the moment they saw the pinto that he was a stranger and a potential enemy. But on the sorrel he might pass for one of them. Long enough to reach Paradise alive, at any rate. He explained it to the pair as he forked leather.

"Take care," Mary Beth said earnestly.

Fargo rode eastward sixty feet and then kneed the sorrel up out of the gully. Tucking his chin to his chest, he boldly trotted toward the den of iniquity. He saw no lookouts but they were likely to be hidden from view. From under his hat brim he studied how the buildings were laid out.

The largest, a barn or stable, sat to the north. It was the most rundown of all, with planks missing from the sides and part of the roof gone. Built long ago, the structures had taken a stiff beating from the elements. Two smaller buildings were next to it. One was a frame house, as out of place in the Badlands as a palace or castle would be. The other was little more than a shack, but the roof and walls were still intact. The house was at the foot of the cliff, the shack was across from it.

Next in line was the second-largest structure, a long, low affair. From it tinkled music and rowdy laughter, and from its chimney rose the smoke Fargo had spotted earlier. The last two buildings were shoddy cabins built with logs, planks, and big stones, seemingly from whatever had been handy at the time. Finally, off by itself, sat the outhouse.

Not a soul was abroad. Nor were any horses tied to either of the two hitching posts. To all appearances Paradise was a ghost town, only belied by the racket coming from what must be the saloon.

Fargo approached the largest building. The double doors were wide open, the door on the right hanging by a single hinge. From inside wafted the scent of recently cut hay, along with the less fragrant scent of horse droppings. Fargo reined up in the doorway. A huge pile of grass was just inside, to the right.

Horses packed the dilapidated excuse for a stable. Dozens lined the sides, more were in stalls. The outlaws had placed all their eggs, as it were, in one basket. Fargo smiled. When the time came, he could drive the animals off and leave the outlaws stranded.

"Buenas tardes, amigo."

From out of the shadows on the left ambled a tall bearded Mexican wearing a sombrero and poncho. He had been seated in an old rocking chair in the corner. Under his left arm a rifle was cradled.

Fargo tensed, then willed himself to relax, to act as if he belonged there. Recollecting what Mary Beth had told him about the attack on her family, he said, "Is that you, Juan?"

The man in the poncho laughed and responded in clipped English. "Are you loco, friend? It is I, Pedro Hernandez. How could you mistake me for that runt?" He was facing the doorway and had to squint against the glare, which worked in Fargo's favor.

"Will you take care of my horse?" Fargo asked, sliding down.

Pedro chuckled. "You are a funny man, señor. First you think I am Juan. Now you want me to tend to your animal? Do I look like your servant? Or one of the women? Take care of your own, eh?"

Fargo had his palm on the butt of the Colt. "I was just joshing you," he said, and started to lead the sorrel further in.

The Mexican pointed at a stall. "That one is not being used at the moment."

"I'm obliged," Fargo said. Spinning, he slugged Pedro across the skull. The guard buckled without a sound, his sombrero falling off. Quickly, Fargo bent and dragged Pedro into the corner. Removing the poncho, Fargo donned it, then the sombrero. He turned to the tack hanging on the wall, including bridles. A few slashes with the Arkansas toothpick and Fargo had enough leather strips to bind Pedro hand and foot.

Instead of putting the sorrel in the stall, Fargo tied it near the entrance, handy for a swift getaway. His hat went over the saddle horn. Sliding his hands under the poncho, he sauntered outdoors, his head held low so his features were concealed.

The saloon was his destination. He was almost abreast of the frame house when the front door opened and out walked a pair of women in tight, gaudy dresses. They moved slowly, stiffly, their faces gaunt, their eyes haunted. It was as if all their zest for life had been drained, as if they were empty husks, mere shells of human beings. Fargo slowed so they wouldn't get a good look at him. The foremost, a raven-haired broomstick who once might have been beautiful, looked around.

"Hello, Pedro."

"Hola," Fargo said, doing his best to sound like the Mexican. *"Cómo está usted?"*

The woman mustered a feeble grin. "Why do you always tease me? You know I don't speak Spanish."

"How are you?" Fargo asked, contriving to cough as he did, to mask his voice.

"Lousy, as usual," the woman said. "Another day in hell, courtesy of you and the rest of the demons."

The other woman recoiled and glanced at Fargo in mortal fear. "Hush, Louise. He'll tell on you. They'll beat you or make you spend a day in the box."

Louise shrugged. "So? I honestly don't care anymore, Martha. I'd rather die than go on as they make us do. At their beck and call twenty-four hours a day. Always being pawed over. Treated like their personal playthings."

"Bite your tongue," Martha advised.

"I'm sick and tired of living in fear," Louise said. "Sick to my soul of spending half of every day flat on my back! I don't deserve this." She snatched her wrist back when her friend tried to grasp it. "I had a loving husband! I was happy! Content! And now look! Bill is dead and I'm a—a—" Unable to bring herself to say the word, Louise burst into tears and covered her face with her hands.

Fargo had heard enough. These women were victims of the same savagery that had resulted in Ed Webber's murder and Esther's abduction. He started toward them, to whisper that their ordeal would soon be over, that he was there to help get them out. But as he raised his chin, the one called Martha looked past him, toward the shack across from the house. Her eyes grew wide with fright and she seized Louise and whispered urgently in the other woman's ear.

"What is going on here? Why do you cry, white squaw?" said a voice from behind Fargo.

Being careful not to show his face, Fargo swiveled. The newcomer was a swarthy man, part Indian, with greasy black hair and bushy dark brows. He wore long pants and had a breechcloth on over them. On his right hip was a Remington, on his left a bowie.

It was the half-breed who had killed Mary's father, Fargo guessed. And he was right.

"We're fine, Coletto," Martha said timidly. "Louise just has a case of the sniffles, is all. Sorry if we bothered you."

In front of the shack, in the shade by the closed door, was an old wooden crate. Coletto had been perched on it, and Fargo was annoyed he hadn't noticed sooner. Now Coletto glared at the two women. "You do not like doing what we say? Maybe you should have a talk with Juan or the boss."

Martha reacted as if the half-breed had plunged cold steel into her heart. "No! No! We're fine! Honest! Give us a minute, will you? Louise hasn't been feeling well lately."

"Is that so?" Coletto said sarcastically.

Louise surprised everyone by whirling and jabbing a finger at him. "No, it's not!" she declared, tears streaking her cheeks. "I'm crying because I hate what you've done to me! I hate Paradise! I hate you and the rest of the scum who ride with you! But most of all, I hate living!"

Martha wrapped an arm around her friend's shoulders and hastily pulled her away. "Quiet! For the love of God! He'll kill us!"

But Coletto threw back his head and laughed. He enjoyed their suffering. He reveled in their misery. Fargo had met men like the half-breed before, men in whom there wasn't a shred of human decency. "I will not waste the bullets. All you whites are weak, so go ahead and cry to your room."

Eager to comply, Martha headed for the saloon but Louise

tore loose and made as if to tear into her tormentor. "I hope to hell you get yours, soon! I hope to hell your body rots, and maggots eat what's left! You're a miserable son of a bitch, Coletto!"

The half-breed was on them in a bound. His brawny hand flashed out, whipcord tough, and smacked Louise across the cheek so hard, her skin split from her chin to her ear. "Still your tongue, squaw! Or I will give you more cause to hate me."

"I dare you!" Louise spat, crimson rivulets seeping between the hand she had clasped to her cheek. "You're just like all the others! A coward, unless you run in a pack!"

The bowie leaped from its sheath in a blur. Fargo took a step but he was much too slow. The keen edge bit into Louise just above the elbow. Not deep, but deep enough to draw blood. Louise cried out and staggered back. Martha uttered a scream, then stifled it by clamping both hands over her mouth.

Chortling sadistically, Coletto wagged the bowie, crimson drops dripping from its tip. "Run, white squaws! Run, or I will give you your wish!" He pretended to pounce and the women fled toward the saloon, whimpering and clinging to one another in terror. "You see that, Pedro?" Coletto said. "White women are cattle."

"*Sí,*" Fargo said, hurrying past before the half-breed saw through his disguise. When he was almost to the saloon, Fargo glanced back. Coletto had returned to the crate, but he was staring at him intently. It did not bode well.

Martha and Louise had halted, and Martha was examining her friend's wounds. "You brought it on yourself," she was saying. "You should have kept your fool mouth shut." They regarded Fargo as if he were a slimy slug.

Skirting them, Fargo opened the saloon door. Noise, smoke, and the odor of liquor buffeted him. He slipped inside, his back to the left-hand wall, waiting for his eyes to adjust. Only two windows admitted light, and it was like stepping into a cave. Close to thirty people were at the bar, playing poker, or milling. The majority were gruff men cut from the same coarse cloth as Pedro and Coletto. In the far corner was a piano long past its prime, and playing it was a woman whose frame was bent in abject sorrow.

Fargo had found Esther Webber.

9

The saloon was stifling hot. As well it should be, given that the haunches of a deer were roasting in the fireplace. All the burlap flaps over the windows had been tied back to let in the breeze, but it did little to provide relief. The patrons didn't seem to mind. It gave them an excuse to drink more.

As Skye Fargo laid eyes on Esther, she slumped and bowed her head in despair. A short, hefty Mexican wearing twin ivory-handled Smith & Wessons jangled from the bar and stood next to her. "Did I say you could stop, *puta*?" he demanded, cuffing her on the ear. "Keep playing."

"I'm so tired I can't think," Esther said bleakly. "You haven't let me sleep, you won't let me eat. Please. In God's name. Show some human decency."

Many of the outlaws had stopped what they were doing to watch. They laughed uproariously when Juan suddenly hit Esther with sufficient force to knock her to the floor. "Bitch! You will sleep when I say, eat when I say! Now play, or I will let Coletto amuse himself with your daughter."

Esther looked up, and never in his life had Fargo beheld a face so lined by abject suffering, so filled with rank misery. Yet she refused to give up; she refused to be overwhelmed by her anguish and grief. Fargo saw her marshal her energy and sit up, admiring how she struggled to her feet and sat on the bench. He knew she was doing it for Claire's sake, and that Esther's motherly love was all that kept her going.

"I'll do anything you want so long as you don't hurt my little girl."

Juan gripped her chin. "How noble you are, eh? White worm! You disgust me!" The *pistolero* spat in her face, provoking general mirth. "I know your kind. You think that you are so much better than us. That we are no more than filthy animals. Am I right?" When Esther didn't answer, Juan shook her like a terrier shaking a rabbit. "Gringos! Always looking down their noses at me! If you weren't so valuable to us, I would gut you like a fish and strangle you with your own intestines."

Esther suffered the abuse in stoic silence. He pushed her but she stayed on the seat.

"Now play!" Juan barked. "And don't stop again unless I tell you to." Rotating on a boot heel, the bantam badman stalked from the saloon.

Fargo was well away from the door, in deep shadow. As soon as it closed, he sidled along the wall, keeping his head low, until he was near the piano. Esther's fingers roved indifferently over the keys. How she could see to play anything, with tears flowing nonstop, was beyond him. No one was paying attention to her now, so Fargo felt safe in moving closer still with his back to the room. Bending, he whispered in her ear, "Whatever you do, don't let on that you know me. I'm here to get Claire and you out."

Despite his warning, Esther was so startled that she hit the wrong keys. The jarring notes brought a few heads up. To her credit, Esther quickly recovered and resumed playing. "Skye? Is it really you?" she whispered back.

"Where do they have your daughter?"

Esther was crying harder, her lips quivering, her forearms starting to shake. If she wasn't careful, Fargo worried, she would give him away. Hoping no one was close enough to observe what he was doing, Fargo gently placed a hand on her shoulder. "Be strong, for your daughter's sake. Mary is safe. Now all we need to do is take Claire and you to join her."

"Mary—safe?" Esther glanced at him, her face shining with gratitude.

Behind Fargo a chair scraped. Removing his hand, he said

loudly in his best imitation of Pedro, "Do as Juan told you!" He sensed someone was right behind him, then smelled fetid breath.

"Keep the bitch in her place, Pedro," a man complimented him. "But if you ask me, she won't last two months once she's auctioned off. Whether Quimico or Diaz gets her won't matter. She doesn't have what it takes."

"*Sí,*" Fargo said.

"I'm glad we've got five other women," the man said. "The bidding should be lively this time around. And that blond filly Pearson is bringing should fetch one of the highest prices ever, according to the boss. She's a real looker."

Fargo felt that to stay silent might make the hard case wonder, so he said, "The more money, the better for us."

"Got that right, amigo. Our share from this batch should be two hundred dollars each. Maybe three hundred if Quimico takes a shine to the kids. Diaz never buys them."

"That is a lot of money."

"More than I've ever had at one time in all my born days." The gunman chuckled. "Maybe I'll call it quits and head for Denver. I hear the women up there are fresh as daisies. They take baths at least once a week, and put on new clothes every day. Why, I'd pay just to *smell* them."

A hand clapped Fargo on the back. Tilting his head so the sombrero concealed his features, he watched the swarthy cutthroat amble to the bar. The news about Quimico and Diaz was disturbing. Two of the most brutal men alive were on their way to Paradise, and neither would come alone. Quimico's band, the last Fargo had heard, numbered over a dozen, and General Diaz was bound to bring about the same number of soldiers. A larger force was more likely to be detected, and the American government wouldn't take kindly to having a foreign military power intrude on its sovereign soil.

Fargo had to hand it to the leader of the outlaws—whether it was Vetch or someone else. The idea of an auction was brilliant. But then, so was each step of the scheme. Picking pilgrims who had been foolish enough to try and cross the prairie alone or who had been separated from their wagon trains. Luring them into the Badlands with the promise of a glorious new life in Paradise. Killing the men, taking the women captive. Selling the females to the highest bidder. And the whole thing had been worked out so there was little risk to the mastermind and those who worked for him. Whoever was behind it wasn't a run-of-the-mill outlaw.

Fargo leaned over Esther. "Where's Claire?" he asked again.

Esther answered without turning her head. "In the next building to the north. Be careful, though. It's guarded by a wicked man who is part Indian."

Coletto, Fargo realized. So that was why the half-breed had been sitting in front of the shack. "I can't take you with me just yet. But once your daughter is safe, I'm coming back. Don't give up hope."

"I'm not worried anymore," Esther said cheerfully. "She's been right about you all along."

"Who?"

"Claire. She's been insisting that you're our guardian angel. I thought it was childish fancy. Now I see I was mistaken. You really are."

Fargo couldn't believe she was serious, but she was. He figured the stress and the lack of rest and food were to blame. She simply wasn't thinking straight, a point he didn't bother mentioning. "You'll be all right until I return?"

"I'm fine now," Esther said lightheartedly. "Honest. Do what you have to."

Giving her a squeeze, Fargo pivoted and headed for the door. He hugged the wall, his hands under the poncho, taking his sweet time as the real Pedro would. He even stopped to observe a poker game in progress. No one challenged him. No one tried to stop him. Shoving out the door, he bore to the right. At the corner he paused to scour the dusty street. None of the denizens were abroad. That included Coletto. The crate in front of the shack was empty.

Hastening on around the saloon, Fargo halted at the rear.

Piles of trash and refuse stank to high heaven. Threading through them, he passed the back door, which was ajar. Through it, he glimpsed a narrow hallway and two outlaws. Neither noticed him. Walking faster, he came to the shack. Part of a filthy sheet had been tacked over the window. Drawing the Arkansas toothpick, Fargo cut a small hole and rose on his toes to place his right eye to it. Directly under him lay a woman, bound ankles and wrists, a gag over her mouth. The legs of another were visible, likewise bound.

Replacing the knife, Fargo ran to the front. Coletto was still gone, the street still deserted. Fargo dashed to the door and worked the wooden latch. He was inside in the bat of an eye, closing the door behind him. Just as the man in the saloon had said, there were five women. And they weren't the only captives. In an opposite corner huddled Claire Webber, her face averted, trembling in terror. Fargo started toward the child, then saw who was across from her. Shock stopped him in midstride. "You?" he blurted.

All Cyrus Vetch could do was nod. Tied and gagged, he was on his side, his bowler in front of him.

"I'll have all of you free in a minute," Fargo announced. Several of the women tried to speak, their words too muffled to understand, and began bobbing their heads like a flock of demented chickens. He motioned for them to be still. "Quiet, or the outlaws will hear."

Claire hadn't moved. Sinking to a knee, Fargo placed a hand on her arm. She jumped and whimpered like a puppy. "It's me, Skye," he said softly.

The girl seemed not to hear. She pressed against the planks, and when Fargo attempted to pry her away, she balked. Precious time was being lost. "Claire?" Fargo said, and felt like a fool saying what he did next. "Don't you remember your guardian angel?"

The child roused. Seeing him, Claire commenced crying tears of sheer joy. She let Fargo take her into his arms.

"Everything will be fine now, little one."

The women were pumping their bound arms and legs and

rolling back and forth. Each wanted to be the first one freed, Fargo reckoned. He undid the knots at Claire's wrists and legs, then set her down and moved to Cyrus Vetch. Two people could untie everyone faster than one. As he reached for Vetch's gag, the women grew frantic. "Wait your turn!" he whispered sternly.

Vetch sat up. He looked at each of the women and they calmed down. After the strip of cloth was removed from his mouth, he smiled and sucked in deep breaths. "Thanks, friend. It's stifling in here. I could hardly breathe."

"I never expected to find you a prisoner," Fargo mentioned. He still didn't completely trust the man. It was Vetch, after all, who had lured the Webbers to Paradise.

"I've been held against my will for over six months now," Cyrus said. "Juan and those riffraff use me to trick poor souls like the Webbers into entering the Badlands."

"Juan is the leader?"

"No, there's someone higher up," Vetch said. "Someone I've never met." He thrust his wrists at Fargo. "Hurry, please. If they catch us, my daughter's life is forfeit. They have her in the house across the street. It's how they bend me to their will. If I don't obey, they'll murder her."

So that was it. Fargo should have guessed as much. Vetch was just another victim. The outlaws needed someone who looked perfectly harmless, someone who could ride up to a settler's wagon without being shot on sight. Juan and Coletto certainly couldn't. Fargo swiftly freed Vetch and said, "Give me a hand."

Cyrus slid to the first woman, who cringed at his touch until he smacked her on the hip. "Quit acting a fool, Julia. You know what has to be done."

Claire was staring wide-eyed at Fargo. She had gone strangely rigid and didn't utter a sound when he picked her up. "In ten minutes you'll be with your big sister, Mary."

"The older daughter is with you?" Vetch said. "What about the four men who were left at the wagon to hunt her down?"

"About now they're making the buzzards happy."

"You don't say?" Cyrus moved to another captive. "You must be one tough hombre, friend. Ike Pearson and those others weren't slouches."

"I get by."

In short order the women were all helped to their feet. They were composed but scared, bunched together in the middle of the room. Fargo produced the Colt and glided to the door. "We're going straight to the stable. Stay close and don't look back."

"I'll go last to protect them," Vetch offered. "Not that I can do much good without a gun.

Cracking the door open, Fargo confirmed Coletto hadn't returned. Beckoning, he stepped outside. No cries rang out as he ushered his frightened flock toward the wide doors. He had to resist an urge to run, which would alert anyone who spotted them. Claire had her small arms around his neck, her face buried in his neck.

To the south, a dull drumming broke out.

Fargo turned and felt his mouth go dry. A cloud of dust signaled the arrival of riders who weren't quite in sight yet. More outlaws, he figured, and threw caution aside. "Move!" he commanded. The dust cloud swelling rapidly, they hustled into the stable just in time.

With Vetch at his elbow, Fargo peeked out and counted fifteen horsemen strung out in a ragged line.

In the lead was a tall man, the taint of cruelty indelibly stamped on his features. A hawkish profile, a hooked nose, and a jutting chin all contributed to the veiled violence that hung over him like an ominous thundercloud. A red headband adorned his shoulder-length black hair. His clothes were Mexican in style, a black shirt and pants with flared bottoms, and black boots inlaid with silver curlicues and swirls. He favored a Sharps rifle as well as a Remington revolver.

"Quimico!" Cyrus Vetch exclaimed. "He's early!"

"You've met him?"

"He's been here before. A more dangerous fellow you'll never meet. It was my understanding he wasn't due for an-

107

other week. He must be chomping at the bit to get his hands on some new women. He goes through them like some men go through ammunition."

"The ladies he buys at the auctions?"

"You know about them?" Vetch nodded and squatted. "They've been taking place for a year and a half. Every three months, like clockwork, anywhere from five to a dozen women are sold off. Quimico is always here. Another regular is a Mexican officer from the state of Sonora—"

"General Diaz."

Vetch glanced up sharply. "You know about him, too? Damn. Is there anything you *don't* know?"

"Why men like Quimico and Diaz would come all this way to buy women when they can take any one they want, any time they want."

"Oh, that's simple. Sure, Quimico could swoop down on a ranch and help himself. Only then he'd have all the ranchers for a hundred miles around after him, to say nothing of the U.S. Army. It's the same with Diaz. He can have his pick of any woman in Sonora. But nine times out of ten they have relatives, a husband, a brother, a father, you name it, who will try to get even." Vetch paused. "So Quimico and Diaz are more than willing to ride a few hundred miles for convenience's sake. They know that every female they buy here is theirs, free and clear. No one will ever hound them over it. They can do as they please without having to look over their shoulders." Vetch paused again. "Besides which, General Diaz is partial to white women. They say he tortures them for hours on end."

One of the captives, a brunette whose face was smeared with grime and whose dress was a tattered mess, cleared her throat as if to say something. But when Fargo and Vetch looked at her, she looked away.

"These poor women have been here so long, they're afraid of their own shadows," Vetch said. "They're beaten if they so much as look at someone wrong. But not hard, mind you. Bruises and blemishes lower the asking price."

Fargo thought of Martha and Louise, and nodded at the frame house. "What about the women over there?"

"They're the ones who weren't pretty enough to interest the buyers. The outlaws need companionship, too." Vetch gazed at Quimico's band, who were almost to Paradise. "What rotten timing. This could ruin everything."

Cutthroats were spilling from the saloon. Juan was with them, and he moved to the front to greet the newcomers. That the outlaws didn't trust the renegades was demonstrated by a show of rifles and hands nervously placed on pistol butts.

Quimico slowed forty yards out and advanced warily, the Sharps cocked and resting across his thighs. His beady eyes flicked back and forth like a snake's forked tongue. Some women were in the doorway to the saloon and his gaze hungrily lingered on them.

"Juan should know better than to let those girls show themselves," Vetch remarked. "It could cause trouble."

The second-in-command was waiting with his arms folded, his sombrero pushed back. He raised a hand in greeting and Quimico did likewise. As the renegades reined up, Juan strode to Quimico's bay.

"What the hell is she doing?" Vetch suddenly snapped.

A figure had appeared in the saloon window facing the shack. Fargo recognized Esther Webber. She hooked a leg over the bottom and clambered out, nearly falling. Her dress snagged and she had to tug to rip it loose. Slinking to the front, she stared at the parley taking place. All the people from the saloon were looking the other way.

Fargo knew what she was going to do and came close to showing himself. He had to warn her not to try. She risked ruining everything.

Then Esther moved into the open, toward the shack. She figured no one would notice, that with everyone interested in the renegades, she could move about freely. Reaching the shack, she opened the door and took a quick look inside. Beaming, Esther whirled toward the stable.

The abrupt movement caught the eagle eye of Quimico. He said something to Juan, who pivoted.

"Damn it to hell!" Cyrus Vetch declared. "We'll be found out because of her."

"She wants Claire," Fargo said in Esther's defense. "Any mother would do the same."

At the mention of her mother, Claire raised up. Her eyes lit up like torches and she went to shout.

"No!" Fargo said, pressing a hand over the child's mouth. One yell would be their downfall. Claire struggled, biting him, but he wouldn't let go. Lowering his head, he whispered, "If you shout, the badmen will catch us and put us back in the shack. Is that what you want?"

Vetch had not taken his eyes off Esther. "They're on to her. She'll never reach the stable."

A fierce whoop echoed off the cliff. Quimico jabbed his spurs into the bay and galloped into the midst of the outlaws, scattering gunmen right and left. Esther looked over a shoulder, saw him coming, and ran faster. But no one could outrun a horse. She covered another twenty feet, then had to dodge aside as Quimico swept past and cut the bay in front of her.

"No!" Esther cried, swatting at the bandit's leg.

Quimico sneered and kicked her, nearly bowling Esther over. She darted to the right to go around when Quimico reined the horse in a tight arc, thwarting her. Reversing direction, Esther darted to the left. With the same result. Again and again she sought to flee, but the renegade, exhibiting masterly control over his mount, headed her off at every turn.

The outlaws and Quimico's men flocked down the street to witness the fun. Most were laughing at Esther's expense, enjoying her plight. Even a few of the women cackled and slapped their thighs.

"She would have been better off staying in the saloon," Vetch coldly commented.

Claire was beside herself, fighting to break Fargo's hold. "There's nothing we can do," he whispered. "Please, calm down." But she refused. Kicking and pushing, she battled like a wildcat.

Cyrus twisted his head. "Give her a slap. That should quiet her down."

Fargo would rather slap Vetch. How could the man be so callous? He moved away from the door to spare Claire the inevitable outcome. The child's blows were weakening, her tears a downpour. She looked at him with such hurt in her eyes, he withered. "There are too many," he said. "There's nothing I can do."

A screech from the street brought the uproar to an end. Fargo had to see. Esther was in Quimico's grasp and had been yanked partially up over the saddle. She jerked her face away when he tried to kiss her. Sneering, the killer extended his tongue and licked her from her chin to her ear. Then he shoved her to the ground.

Claire mewed and sniffled.

"I'm sorry," Fargo said. And he had never been more so.

Rough hands seized Esther Webber. Slung between two stocky outlaws, she was summarily hauled off. The entertainment over with, most of the outlaws filed into their haven. Quimico and Juan consulted, and presently the killer led his pack to the southeast.

"He likes to make camp up on the cliff," Vetch revealed. "Claims he feels safer up there because no one can sneak up on him. I guess if I had as many bounties on my head as he does, I'd do the same."

Somewhere or other Fargo had heard that over five thousand dollars had been posted on Quimico, dead or alive. The rest of his band had lesser amounts, but every one was wanted either in the U.S. or Mexico, or both countries. They were as deadly a bunch as ever drew breath, and few bounty hunters had the sand to go after them. The last one to try wound up skinned alive and staked out over a mound of red ants. Upset at how long the ants were taking to finish the bounty hunter off—so the story went—Quimico had his men collect a basket full of scorpions and poured them over him.

In a surprisingly short time, Paradise's sole street was empty once more. Vetch rose and went down the center aisle. "I'll fetch the horses we'll need."

Fargo gently set Claire down and took his hand away. She stared at him in that hurt manner of hers, not speaking, not needing to. "If there had been any other way—" he said lamely. The girl's hurt deepened.

"You're an angel. You can do anything. You should have saved her."

What was Fargo to say? That he wasn't an angel, that he'd never seen an angel and never known anyone who had? That it was silly of her to believe he was something he wasn't. That it was time she started to grow up? Instead, he said, "If I'd tried anything, those men would have killed her."

"You will save Ma, though? You won't let them harm her?"

"I'll try my best."

Satisfied, the girl grinned. "I knew I could trust you. Ma says angels never let us down. I'm sorry I acted up."

Saddling enough mounts for all of them took almost twenty minutes. Fargo and Vetch had to work quietly, one or the other always on guard. Fortunately, none of the outlaws came to the stable. In fact, no one appeared on the street the whole time. The women climbed on when Fargo instructed them to, then he forked the sorrel, pulling Claire up in front of him.

"How do you aim to do this?" Vetch was curious. "Ride like hell and pray they don't catch us?"

"And have them hear us?" Fargo responded. "No. We'll do it slowly, one at a time, in single file. No talking. Not a peep unless we're jumped."

Riding from the stable, Fargo bore to the west. No living creature moved anywhere in Paradise. Even the sluggish breeze had died. Escaping was ridiculously easy. Crossing the valley was no more challenging than crossing a city park. As they neared the gully, Mary and George Lyndon showed themselves, Mary rushing to greet her sister.

"So there they are," Cyrus Vetch said, bringing his horse up beside the sorrel as the whole party came to a stop. "I can't thank you enough."

"For saving you?" Fargo said.

"No, for tying up the loose ends." From under Vetch's gray jacket slid his left hand, and in it was a pistol.

10

In his bowler hat and loose gray clothes, with his round face and bulbous nose, the pudgy man called Cyrus Vetch had always seemed more comical than dangerous. Until now. Vetch had undergone a change, a transformation. He was less like a roly-poly clown and more like a burly wolverine, a flinty glitter in his flat eyes, his teeth bared as if to bite and tear instead of curled in his usual smile. His hand rose, the hammer of his Whitney 5-shot .31-caliber pocket revolver clicking back.

Skye Fargo told himself he shouldn't be surprised, but he was. Although he had never entirely trusted Vetch, their last hour together had dulled his suspicions. Now he saw the sequence of events in a new light. "The whole thing was a trap to catch Mary and me?"

"Quite an elaborate trap, if I do say so myself," Vetch boasted. "But my intellect has always been the equal of any occasion."

"So you *are* the boss? The ringleader of the whole operation?"

"At your service," Vetch said with mock humility and a tiny bow. His gaze drifted to George Lyndon and the Whitney swiveled. "I don't know you, mister, but I'd suggest you put down that shotgun before I put a slug between your eyes. Believe me. You'd never know it to look at me, but I'm an excellent shot. I rarely miss."

Lyndon was rooted where he stood, stunned by the revelation. Fargo couldn't predict what he would do. Here was the person George had been searching months for, the mastermind responsible for the loss of his son and his daughter-in-law. The man George was primed to slay on sight. Yet if he cut loose, Fargo would be caught in the spray of buckshot.

"At last!" Lyndon declared. "You're the son of a bitch I've dreamed of killing for more nights than I can remember!"

"Is that so?" Vetch said, unconcerned. "I'm flattered. What did I do to deserve such hatred?"

George took a step, his face reddening. "Does the name Robert Lyndon ring a bell? He was my son, and he disappeared along with his wife, Susan. The last I heard from them, *you* were acting as their guide, leading them to Paradise."

Vetch pursed his thick lips. "Ah. So he got a letter out, did he? I'd thought as much, but it couldn't be prevented." Vetch's trigger finger was slowly tightening. "Your son is dead, old man. Killed by an associate of mine, Coletto, when he tried to stop us from taking his wife. He fought well, if it's any consolation. But that half-breed is a marvel with a knife."

"Dead," Lyndon said, dazed, the confirmation destroying his last shred of hope.

"As for Susan, she was bought by a renegade named Quimico. From what I understand, she only lived a couple of months. Stupid bitch wouldn't do as Quimico wanted. So one day he had her hung upside down from a tree and slit her throat over a bucket to collect the blood, which he mixed with the slop being fed to some pigs his men had stolen. To add to the flavor when he ate them, was how he explained it to me."

Fargo had to do something. Anything. Horror and loathing were contorting George's features. At any instant George would try to blow Vetch in half. He couldn't get out of the way in time. And if he tried to unlimber his Colt or to jump Vetch, the pudgy monster was bound to put a slug into him. Lyndon was so agitated, he'd fire anyway, killing both of them. "George," he said, "do as the man wants and lower your cannon. For my sake."

"You heard him, Skye! He's admitted it! The whole thing!"

"I know. But I also know this isn't the right time. Set down the shotgun, George. Please."

115

Lyndon was not going to do any such thing. Everyone there could tell. Fury danced on his brow and his body was tensed like a steel spring. "You murdered my Robert!" he roared, and up came the shotgun.

All Cyrus Vetch had to do was squeeze. The Whitney belched lead and smoke. A .31-caliber slug caught George Lyndon in the center of his forehead, the slug coring his skull and rupturing out the rear of his cranium.

Simultaneously, Fargo threw himself at Vetch. He dove from the saddle, careful not to upend Claire, and he was already in midair when Vetch shifted and swung the Whitney toward him. It went off. Fargo felt a prick along his ribs, no more severe than the scrape of a pin. Then he slammed into Vetch, spilling the pudgy man from the saddle and bearing both of them to earth.

They hit on the lip of the gully. For such a short, heavyset man, Cyrus Vetch was uncommonly strong. He sought to shove the Whitney against Fargo's body and fire again but Fargo had a grip on Vetch's wrist and held the pistol away. They grappled, rolling back and forth, until they suddenly hurtled over the brink and tumbled. They came to a jarring rest at the bottom in a tiny cloud of dust.

Vetch's icy bearing was gone. Wrath oozed from every pore, his face like that of a maddened beast. Spearing fingers at Fargo's eyes, he sought to rake them with his thick dirty nails. Fargo twisted and had his cheek scraped open, instead. A knee rammed into his thigh. He heaved, flinging Vetch onto his back, then pounced, thinking to pin the killer. But Vetch's foot drove up into his gut, upending him, and he wound up on his own back. They were side by side, joined where their hands were clamped on the Whitney.

"You bastard!" Vetch snarled, punching at Fargo's throat. "No one has ever given me so much damn trouble!"

Fargo blocked the blow and delivered one of his own to Vetch's well-padded chin. It snapped Vetch's head back but the man wasn't one of those with a glass jaw. Unfazed, Vetch struck Fargo on the temple, and again on the neck.

"I'm going to relish slaying you!"

Fargo grabbed Vetch's gun hand with both of his own, then smashed Vetch's wrist against a rock, seeking to make Vetch release the Whitney, or at least weaken Vetch's grip so he could tear the revolver free. But inside the flabby body of Cyrus Vetch lurked a will of iron. Vetch clung on and they surged back and forth, trading more punches and kicks.

Neither could gain the upper hand. They rolled against a boulder and Fargo found himself wedged against it with little room to move. Vetch kneed him in the groin, then in the stomach. Fargo deflected more blows by shifting sideways.

The Whitney was trapped between their chests, the barrel angled upward. "Prepare to die!" Vetch declared, his confidence out of all proportion to his size and shape. Yet it was not entirely unfounded. For slowly, inexorably, he began to tilt the barrel toward Fargo's face.

There was movement around them but Fargo couldn't take his eyes off Vetch to see what caused it. Shoulders rippling, he resisted the pressure on the revolver. Vetch was so intent on putting a slug into him that the man had stopped trying to knee his groin. In the lull, Fargo arced his own knee into where it would have the most telling effect.

Wheezing, Vetch turned several shades of purple. His grip slackened long enough for Fargo to gain sole possession of the Whitney. As Vetch lunged to reclaim it, Fargo brought it crashing down on the man's brow. It slowed Vetch, but didn't stop him. Gripping Fargo's wrist, he thrust his other hand at Fargo's jugular.

Fargo heaved away from the boulder, throwing all his weight into it and rolling on top of Vetch. They were nose to nose, the ruthless mastermind still concentrating on the Whitney. Fargo brought his forehead smashing down into his foe's mouth, and Vetch shrieked like an outraged alley cat. Again Fargo butted him, and then a third time.

Abruptly, Cyrus Vetch went briefly limp. It lasted long enough for Fargo to wrench loose and shove to his feet. In his haste, though, he tripped. Vetch, swearing, surged up after him.

Out of nowhere they came. The five women captives, all with big rocks in their hands. They were on Vetch before he could lift a finger to defend himself, raining their rocks on his face, his head, his body. He staggered backward and they pressed in close, battering, pummeling, pounding on him again and again. They had him surrounded. No matter which way he turned, a female vision of vengeance reared before him. He raised both forearms to ward off their onslaught but he couldn't ward off all the blows at once. For every one he blocked, four connected.

No one could withstand such a beating. Vetch staggered. He tottered. Blood seeped from a score of cuts and gashes. He was on the verge of collapse.

"That's enough," Fargo said. They needed Vetch alive. He might be able to set up a swap, the outlaw leader for Esther Webber.

Only thing was, the five women continued to batter Vetch in a ceaseless barrage. The thud-thud-thud of flesh being pulped was almost sickening. Vetch was too weak to offer more than token resistance, so all their blows were doing damage. Serious damage. Vetch fell to one knee, his left eyebrow split, his nose shattered.

"Enough!" Fargo said, grabbing the nearest woman, a lean lady in a dirty brown dress. In a twinkling she turned on him like a cougar at bay and swung her rock at *him*. Her green eyes flashing with inhuman savagery, she seemed to look through him rather than at him. When he seized her wrist, she came at him tooth and nail. "Stop!" he shouted. "I'm on your side!"

Fargo needn't have bothered. The woman wouldn't be denied. It was as if an inner dam had burst, releasing the rage she had pent up for the abuse and indignities and losses she had suffered. He had to drop the Whitney and grab both her wrists to stop her, and even then she sought to kick him. "Calm down!" he urged, giving her a shake that grated her teeth.

Finally, the woman realized her mistake. The madness drained from her like water from a sieve. "Oh, my word! I'm so sorry! So very sorry! But if you only knew what he's done to us—"

The others! Fargo spun and saw Vetch on the ground, being literally beaten to death. The women were bent over him, their arms flailing, drops of blood splattering all four from toe to chest. "Enough!" Fargo cried, bounding in among them and pushing them to either side. "You'll kill him."

Two of the women came to their senses but the last pair were too incensed to quit. Since Fargo stood in their way, they too turned on him. He had to sidestep a blow that would have reduced his nose to a lump of cartilage. Snagging the woman's arm, he flung her against her friend and the two nearly went down.

Inflamed to a fever pitch by his interference, the pair regained their balance and stalked toward him like twin harpies. Fargo held out his hands, trying another appeal. "I'm the one who saved you, remember?"

Evidently they didn't. Slick rocks clutched tight, they stalked him, determined to do whatever it took to get past him, and at Vetch.

"Listen to me!" Fargo yelled.

At that juncture, aid came from an unexpected source. The other three swooped in, wrapping their arms around the last pair, speaking quickly, soothingly, telling them it was over, that Fargo wasn't their enemy, that "the best is done for."

They were right.

Once Fargo felt safe in turning his back on them, he hunkered beside Vetch. The man was a ruin, caked with blood, his head pitted with holes and scrapes, his gray jacket and pants and his shirt ripped and stained. He was flat on his back, twitching convulsively. The fingers of his right hand had been shattered and bone jutted from a joint. Welts laced his neck except at the base of his throat, where a jagged hole spurted crimson dew.

"Damn it all," Fargo said. Exchanging the ringleader for Esther was out of the question. Vetch's remaining span of life could now be measured in minutes.

Fargo glanced up. George Lyndon lay in a spreading red pool, the shotgun nearby, his quest over once and for all. Claire was in Mary's arms, both staring at Cyrus Vetch without a trace of sympathy.

"Trailsman?" croaked the object of their disdain. Vetch coughed up blood, his mouth moving like that of a fish out of water.

Fargo stared at the monster who had caused so many so much heartache. "You knew who I was all along?"

Vetch nodded, the simple movement provoking a spasm of agony. "Yes," he rasped. "I'd seen you once, in Denver. I knew you would be trouble the moment I saw you ride into that clearing."

"The Webbers told me you were rustling up their supper."

"I was in the trees, with Ira Sanders. He was my link to my men. We were talking about when to jump the family when you showed up. I ordered Ira to bushwhack you. After he failed, I had him lay the trap in the hills."

It was nice to know Fargo's hunch had been right all along. Sanders had lied about everything, to protect Vetch. From the very start, deception had been piled on top of deception to keep him in the dark.

"Later I ordered Ira to track you down. He didn't want to. He claimed there was no need since you were leaving." Another spasm racked his broken form. "When Ira failed to show up in Paradise, I knew it was only a matter of time before you put in an appearance. So I laid another trap."

"You pretended to be a captive."

Vetch grinned. "Clever, no? I warned the women they would be killed if they gave me away. Then I had Juan tie me and gag me so you would think I was being held prisoner."

Fargo remembered how the captives in the cabin had acted, how Vetch only had to look at them to shut them up, how they had recoiled when Vetch undid their ropes. He should have seen the truth sooner. "But what if I never showed up in Paradise?"

"Someone with your reputation? Please, don't insult my intelligence. A man like you wouldn't stand for a child being harmed. I reasoned it would be sooner rather than later."

"You had it all worked out," Fargo said. Vetch had indeed thought of everything, and had allowed for every circumstance except one; for the raging thirst for vengeance of those he had wronged.

"I almost pulled it off, didn't I?" the dying man responded. "Another couple of years and I'd have saved enough to live in luxury the rest of my life." His mouth curved wryly. "Never thought it would end like this. Killed by a bunch of stupid bitches."

A shadow fell across them both. Fargo craned his neck back. It was the woman in the brown dress. In her right hand was the jagged rock she had used to cripple Vetch. "He's done for," Fargo said.

"But not dead yet," she said bitterly. "Why are you talking to him? Why aren't you slitting his throat or putting a bullet in his brain?"

"I've never killed a man when he's down and helpless," Fargo answered.

"Even someone as evil as Vetch?" The woman hefted her rock. "Then you're misguided. Move out of the way and I'll do it myself."

"He'll die anyway in a few minutes."

"Move."

The other women were converging. "He did things to us, mister," the tallest said. "Awful, shameful things. Things no woman can bear. We'll have nightmares for the rest of our lives because of him."

"I want the satisfaction of killing him with my own two hands," said the woman in brown. "I've never hurt a soul before, but I can't let this monster live." She rubbed the blood-smeared edge of her rock across the fingers of her other hand. "I want to feel his life ebb. I want to know he's dead, dead, dead."

Fargo stood. "It won't make you feel any better," he objected.

"How would you know?" the woman said. "You haven't been through the hell we have. You haven't had someone take

121

advantage of you. You weren't touched—" She broke off, choked by emotion.

All five were staring at Vetch. They reminded Fargo of the time a pack of starving wolves had circled an elk and ripped it to bloody ribbons. The women had that same hungry look, only their hunger was of an entirely different sort. He gazed down.

"Don't let them, Trailsman. For God's sake!"

Fargo thought of Ed Webber, of Esther, of Claire bound and terrified. Wheeling, he climbed the slope. "This won't be something you want to see," he said, draping an arm over Mary's shoulder and ushering her into the high grass.

The women were ringing around Cyrus Vetch, closing in on him. "No!" he cried. "Please!" But the man who had never shown mercy to anyone else was now begging for it from those who had none to spare.

Fargo and Mary Beth had gone ten paces when the thud-thud-thudding resumed, the beat as constant as a drum, along with moist, sickly, sucking sounds, mixed with the crunch and crackle of bone and cartilage. Mary shuddered. Thankfully, Claire had fallen asleep in her older sister's arms. Mary put her hands over the child's ears anyway.

Fargo surveyed the valley, puzzled none of Vetch's men had come after him. Maybe the cutthroats were under orders. Maybe they were to wait for Vetch to return, or for a signal of some kind. He also scanned the top of the cliff for telltale signs that Quimico was encamped on the summit, but he saw no smoke or movement.

"I feel so sorry for Mr. Lyndon," Mary said louder than she had to, staring at George. "All those months of torment, all the trouble he went to, and for what? To be murdered by the same man who murdered his son."

Life seldom worked out the way it was supposed to, Fargo mused. Happy endings were for fairy tales.

"Now that he's gone, you'll need someone else to help out," Mary Beth said. "I'll leave Claire with these women and go back into Paradise with you to help get Ma."

"I'm going alone," Fargo said. The first time had been risky enough. Now that the outlaws were on their guard, it would be doubly dangerous. Quimico's presence complicated things even more. Truth to tell, it would be a miracle if he got out alive a second time. But he had given Esther his word, and he was her only hope. He would save her or he would die. It was that simple.

"And what are we supposed to do?" Mary asked. "Hide here?"

The gully was no longer safe. In time, Vetch's men *would* come, and were they to find the women near the body, there would be hell to pay for her. Fargo pointed at a tableland to the west. "I'll take you there. If I don't return in two days, I never will. Ride due north until you strike a wagon trail and follow it to Denver."

"On our own? What about hostiles? Storms?"

"You'll have the shotgun and Vetch's revolver." Fargo glanced at her. She was facing Paradise with a crafty look which she tried to hide by feigning interest in the horizon. He wasn't fooled one bit. She would let him ride off alone, then follow to help him whether he wanted her help or not. "Mount up. We'll head out."

Mary Beth was none too pleased. "Right this moment? Shouldn't we wait for—" She stopped, riveted by something over his shoulder.

Fargo rotated.

The five women were emerging from the gully. They moved stiffly, unnaturally, as if the joints in their arms and legs had been fused solid. In the lead was the woman in brown, her face haunted by the deed she had just done. "The vile devil is dead," she declared with less venom than the occasion called for. Large red drops dripped from her rock, spattering on her leg. She touched her finger to the blood, then pressed the finger against her chin, leaving a bright scarlet mark.

"Are you all right, ma'am?" Mary asked.

"I've never felt better in my whole life," the woman said, and licked the rest of the blood off her finger.

Fargo was glad Claire was asleep. He instructed the women

to climb on their horses, and while they did, he tucked the English shotgun under his arm and dragged George Lyndon's body into the gully. A quick scrutiny of Vetch was enough. Where the man had lain was a pulverized mound of flesh and bone. In contrast, Vetch's bowler, only a few yards away, was untouched.

Shedding the sombrero and the poncho, Fargo climbed on the Ovaro. His own hat was still on the sorrel's saddle horn. Retrieving it, he slid the shotgun into his bedroll, took hold of the reins to the spare horses, and trotted westward.

No one had anything to say. The five women were lifeless specters, in the grip of horror as the full import of what they had done dawned on them. Mary Beth was quiet for Claire's sake.

The tableland was seven miles off. Fargo's intent was to leave the women there and be back in Paradise an hour or so after the sun went down. Under cover of darkness, he would locate Esther and get her out.

Always on the lookout for pursuit, Fargo rode up and down the line to keep the women moving. Nervous energy had kept them on the go since their escape, but now, with Vetch dead, their long captivity made itself felt. They were so tired, most couldn't sit straight. And although the outlaws had fed them regularly, it had never been enough to fill their bellies. The food had usually been poorly cooked anyway, as tasteless as sawdust. So, on top of everything else, they were weak from a lack of proper nourishment.

Halfway to the tableland, as Fargo was encouraging the women along, the one in the brown dress caught his attention.

"I don't believe I've thanked you, sir, for all you did on our behalf. We can never repay you for your kindness."

"There's no need."

"I'm Cynthia Pogue, by the way. Four months ago I was on my way to California with my husband and son. Both were murdered right before my eyes." Cynthia closed hers. "I relive it every waking moment. I keep seeing my John being knifed. I see my darling little Richard—"

"Dwelling on it does you no good," Fargo interrupted.

"I can't help it. They were everything to me. Without them, life is unbearable. Hell on earth, if you will."

"You've lasted this long."

"Please, Mr. Fargo. I stayed alive only because I wanted a chance to do to Cyrus Vetch as he had done to me and mine. Now he's met his just reward. And with my husband and son gone, I'm as empty as a hollow gourd." Cynthia motioned at the others. "All of us are." She inhaled sadly. "What will we do with ourselves? How can we go on?"

"How does anyone?" Fargo rejoined. "You take each day one step at a time."

Cynthia paused for a moment, then smiled, her first since they met. "Handsome as can be, and smart, too. No wonder you remind me of John. He was the sweetest man who ever lived, always looking to lend a helping hand to those in need."

No one had ever accused Fargo of being sweet. As for lending helping hands, after this he would think twice before returning a child's lost doll to its owner. He spurred the Ovaro so he could ride beside the sisters.

"The poor dear is out to the world," Mary Beth commented. "She'll sleep the whole night through, unless I'm mistaken. So will the rest." Mary blinked as if at a sudden idea.

"It will be up to you to stand guard," Fargo said.

"Which suits me fine. I'm too worried about Ma to think of sleeping."

The tableland was mainly rock layered with reddish earth, barren of vegetation except for stunted trees here and there. A wide groove worn by erosion knifed across it, the incline gradual enough for the horses to handle. On a broad spine two-thirds of the way to the summit was a godsend—a small spring.

Fargo called a halt. He helped some of the women down. After slaking their thirst, they curled up on the ground. He offered them pemmican but only Cynthia accepted a piece. The rest were asleep within minutes, and soon she joined them. Fargo gave his bedroll to Mary for Claire to use, then he hiked higher, to a wide ledge. From there Paradise was visible, far in the distance. "Your days are numbered," he said to himself.

"How's that?" Mary Beth came up beside him, holding the shotgun.

"I'll be leaving soon."

The blonde never batted an eye. "What's your hurry?"

11

Skye Fargo glanced at Mary Beth Webber. The invitation in her tone had not been his imagination. She wore an inviting look, as well. Of all the times and places for her to pick! he thought. They were on the run from vicious killers. They had a bunch of grief-stricken women to look after. And he had to leave shortly to save Esther. Leave it to Mary to choose the worst possible moment.

Or had she?

From where Fargo stood he could see the five women and the girl, sound asleep beside the spring. They would be out for hours. Between the tableland and Paradise not so much as a dust devil stirred, so the outlaws weren't after them—yet. And he need not leave for another fifteen to twenty minutes. Plenty of time for what Mary Beth had in mind.

She stepped away from the edge, to the rock wall that towered above them, and leaned the English shotgun against it. "You need rest, too. You've been on the go so long, you should relax a spell." Smiling seductively, she stretched, her breasts thrusting against her dress as if seeking release.

Her ploy was so obvious, Fargo grinned. For someone who was inexperienced, she sure learned fast. And she was about to learn a new lesson; a woman should choose carefully when to stoke a man's hunger.

Fargo went to her and roughly pulled her to him. His mouth fastened on her soft, yielding lips. The suddenness of it took her breath away and excited her immensely. Especially when he cupped her right breast and squeezed it, hard.

"Mmmm, so you do want me?" Mary teased when he drew back.

What man wouldn't? Fargo asked himself. With her wind-blown golden hair, her cherry lips, her lovely face and dazzling eyes, to say nothing of her full, lush figure, she was every man's dream woman made real. "As much as you want me," he admitted, and pulled her to him again, sliding his tongue between her velvety lips.

Fargo's manhood surged. This time he wasn't going to go slow. This time he would give his desire full rein, and to that end, he dipped his left hand between her thighs and rubbed his fingers against her nether mound.

Mary Beth gasped and squirmed. "My goodness, you really *do* want me!"

Moving her backward to the wall, Fargo molded their bodies together. They fit like two halves of the same coin. He was hard where she was soft, the bulge in his pants fitting into the junction of her thighs like a knife into its sheath. She wriggled deliciously as he kneaded both of her breasts, his tongue lathering her soft throat and ears.

"I can't get last night out of my mind." Mary panted. "You made me feel things I've never felt before. And I want to feel them again."

"Is that so?" Fargo responded, then they locked mouths. She was growing hotter to the touch, her back arching when he cupped her buttocks. The fingers of her left hand stroked the back of his neck while her right rubbed his hip and upper leg. She was eager for his maleness, so he grasped her right hand and placed it on his bulge.

At the contact Mary stiffened and exhaled loudly. "Ohhhhh-hhhh."

Fargo unfastened her dress, exposing her globes. The nipples were rigid with desire. When he sucked on one, she groaned louder and vigorously rubbed his manhood. Fargo wrapped his fingers around her breast and teased it, pulling on the nipple as if it were elastic. Mary enjoyed the sensation, enjoyed it a lot, her left leg hooking around his to pull him even closer.

Holding her by the waist, Fargo lowered Mary to the ledge. It was smooth enough to be comfortable and didn't gouge his knees when he knelt between her parted legs. Carnal passion lit her flushed features, enhancing her beauty, her passion mounting when he hiked her dress and plunged his hand under its folds.

"Ah! Yes!" Mary exclaimed as Fargo's fingers brushed her inner thigh. She was on fire, her core molten. Starting above her knees, he caressed her smooth skin in small circles, venturing higher and higher until his knuckles slid across her moist slit. Mary bucked like a bronco, her mouth so full and inviting that he couldn't resist kissing her, tasting her, sucking on her tongue.

There would be none of the lengthy foreplay of their last lovemaking, but some was still in order. Fargo inserted the end of his forefinger into her tunnel. She was wet as rain. Her inner walls quivered. Suddenly he buried the finger deep inside and Mary pumped her wonderful bottom up off the ledge, her thighs opening and closing in erotic reflex.

"Like that, Skye! More! More!"

Adding a second finger, Fargo drove them in and out repeatedly, preparing her for what was to come. Mary Beth tossed her head and dug her nails into his shoulders. His lips found her left nipple, which he flicked and tweaked.

"I can't get enough!"

Mary was heaving upward in a regular rhythm when Fargo lowered his other hand to his gunbelt and loosened the buckle, then did the same with his pants. His manhood burst free, jutting like a lance.

Mary's eyes widened. The night before she had not seen his pole clearly. Now that she did, she couldn't resist placing her hands on it, couldn't resist fondling it as if it were a long-lost treasure. Cooing and sighing, she breathed, "You're so big! So hard! Oh, how I want you inside of me!"

Fargo rubbed the tip over her womanhood. Mary Beth tried to impale herself on him but he drew back, letting her think he was going to prolong their coupling. Then, as she sank down, when she had no reason to expect it, he slammed into her like a steamboat into a gravel bar, spearing into her as far as he could go.

"Ahhhh! Yessssssssssssssssss!"

Mary bit his shoulder to keep from screaming. Fargo held on to her hips for leverage and commenced pounding into her with raw abandon. In and out, over and over. She rose to meet him, her backside matching his tempo. Exquisite pleasure shot through him, a prelude of things to come.

"Faster, Skye! Faster!"

Initially, that had been Fargo's idea—to finish quickly. But the bliss she provoked was worth savoring. He grit his teeth and held his explosion in check. Their bodies were smacking together in a frenzied cadence, her moans were rising in volume, when he thought he heard a nicker from below. He couldn't be sure, but it sounded like the Ovaro.

Fargo tried to concentrate in case the nicker was repeated. He tried to listen intently, to be alert in case it had been a hint of danger. But he was close to the brink, so close he could barely hear anything over the pounding of his temples and the roar of blood in his veins. When Mary's burning lips touched his neck, he felt himself start to explode.

By sheer force of will Fargo held off a little longer. He wanted her to spend first, but if she didn't reach the pinnacle soon, it would be too late. He need not have worried. The very next second Mary cried out and gushed, her inner walls wrapping tight around him as her legs clamped his hips.

"Now! Oh, Skye! Now!"

No prompting was necessary. Fargo simply let himself go, and let nature take its course. The blast of his release was like a keg of black powder going off. All the while, he was driving into her hard enough to split her in two.

Mary mashed herself against him, writhing and grinding. Her eyes wide, she flung her head back and crested the summit of ecstasy.

Together, they floated down to earth and slowly coasted to a stop. Fargo, breathing heavily, felt her hot breath on his ear. He remembered the nicker and started to prop himself on his hands but she enfolded him in her arms and held fast. That was when the whinny was repeated, and this time there was no doubt. It was the stallion. Fargo pulled at her, saying, "Something is wrong. I have to get up."

The voice that answered wasn't Mary's. "Get up slow, white dog, or die."

Icy talons raked Fargo's inside. Holding his arms out from his sides, he twisted. At the end of the ledge stood Coletto holding a leveled Spencer. The half-breed's eyes glittered wickedly as he sidled to the left.

Mary was petrified with fear, so much so, she didn't cover herself or close her legs. She gaped like a fawn mesmerized by a sinuous rattler.

"Can I hitch my pants, at least?" Fargo asked.

Coletto was highly amused by the situation. "I catch you at a bad time, white man?" he taunted. "Maybe I should shoot you now, eh? You die with your pecker hanging out. How'd that be?"

What Fargo felt was irrelevant and they both knew it. He glanced at his gunbelt, just out of reach. It might as well be on the sun for all the good it did him.

"You are lucky, white *bastardo,*" Coletto said. "You get to live awhile yet. Juan will want words with you. So hitch them, if you want. Slowly."

Making no sudden moves, Fargo straightened and pulled his pants up. "You're taking me back to Paradise?" he said to keep the cutthroat talking.

"I found Mr. Vetch," Coletto said, frowning. "That Juan, he was worried. It was taking too long. He sent me to check and I tracked you here."

"On foot?"

"That surprises you, white man? I'm part Kiowa. I can run all day and all night and not tire." Coletto gazed at Mary Beth, ogling her naked legs and higher charms. "You are a pretty one, eh? Prettiest I have seen. Maybe I take a taste before we go. Yellow hair always excites me."

Mary came to her senses and sat up, arranging her dress top and bottom. "Touch me and I'll scratch your eyes out!" She backed against the rock wall, her fingers clawed to do just that.

Coletto grinned. "Good. I like it when women fight. I especially like it when they scratch." Extending his tongue, he rimmed his mouth. "How about you, white girl? You like to be licked? I'm a good licker."

Fargo glanced at her as if worried on her account when he was really noting the exact spot where she had propped the shotgun. It would take two steps to reach it. Plenty of opportunity for the half-breed to put a slug in him.

"The women down below never knew I was there," Coletto bragged. "Only the pinto, it knew. Then I heard noise up here, so I came to see." He had not taken his eyes off Mary. "The sounds I heard, they could only be one thing. I thought to myself, no white man would be so stupid. But this one was."

Fargo was inclined to agree. It *had* been careless on his part. Shifting his weight from one foot to the other, he slid his right leg five or six inches toward the shotgun.

Coletto wasn't fooled one bit. "Go ahead, dumb one. Try. Maybe I shoot your knee out. Maybe I shoot your pecker off. Maybe just an ear. Which do you want to lose?"

Mary Beth was fuming. "Quit trying to scare us! Why don't you kill us and be done with it?"

"Kill a pretty woman like you?" Coletto was genuinely shocked. "Juan would have me burnt alive." He chuckled. "No, we have other uses for pretty women. I'm sure you know what they are." He wagged the Spencer at Fargo. "As for your friend, he will not live long, I think. Not when my friends hear what he did. Mr. Vetch, he was a smart man. They liked him. He was going to line our pockets with much money."

"Vetch was a beast in human guise who preyed on innocents," Mary declared. "He got what he deserved."

"I saw him," Coletto repeated. "No one should die like that. Those women should have their fingers chopped off."

Fargo was girding himself for a lunge at the shotgun. He knew he wouldn't make it. The half-breed wouldn't miss, not that close. But he had to try before Coletto marched him down to the horses, made the women bind him up, and then carted him off.

"How do you know they were to blame?" Mary had asked.

"Do I look as stupid as your friend? I saw the tracks. I saw the bloody rocks. I saw dry blood on their hands." The half-breed snickered. "White women are not the weaklings I thought. It was a death worthy of Apaches." He paused. "Now, enough talk. Walk ahead of me with your arms raised."

Pouting, Mary headed for the slope. She had to pass in front of Fargo, and Coletto watched closely to insure they didn't try anything. As a result, Coletto failed to see the small, sleepy-eyed figure who shuffled into sight. Claire was barely awake, rubbing her eyes and yawning. That changed the instant she beheld the half-breed. Sleep was dispelled by fright so potent, she threw back her head and screamed.

Coletto, startled, glanced around, the Spencer swinging with his body. He saw it was only the child and started to swing back.

In that brief interval, Fargo lurched into motion. Mary Beth had blundered between him and the shotgun so he went after Coletto instead, springing and swatting at the Spencer as the barrel lined up with his body. The rifle boomed, the slug hitting the rock wall. Before Coletto could fire again, Fargo had one hand on the rifle and the other around the half-breed's throat. He pushed with all his might to fling Coletto over the edge, but the killer dug in the soles of his moccasins and stood firm.

"White dog!" Coletto hissed. He whipped the stock up and around. Fargo ducked, then slammed his knee into Coletto's midsection. It had no effect; the half-breed was solid muscle.

Fargo brought his boot crashing down on Coletto's instep. A howl of fury was torn from the man's throat. He hurtled at Fargo, the Spencer forgotten as he drew his bowie and streaked it overhead for a killing stroke.

Fargo had to forget about the Spencer, too. It fell as he flung his right hand up and grabbed Coletto's wrist before the bowie could descend. The killer drove him backward to the middle of

the ledge, where they fought for control of the big knife, Co-
letto growling deep in his barrel chest like a maddened animal.
A clever fighter, the half-breed forked his right leg behind
Fargo, then rammed his shoulder into Fargo's chest.

In a rush of air, Fargo wound up flat on his back. The half-
breed didn't delay a second, stabbing the bowie straight down.
Fargo's upthrust knees saved him. And as he levered them high,
his hand slid into the top of his boot and palmed the Arkansas
toothpick. He kicked Coletto off, rolled, and was in a crouch
with the toothpick held next to his leg when Coletto surged toward him again, swinging the bowie as if it were a sword.

Fargo had to retreat. The weapon that had made its original
wielder famous was rightfully regarded as one of the deadliest
on the frontier. Thicker than most knives, the blade of a bowie
could shear bone as well as flesh. Skipping backward, Fargo
dodged several slashes. Then he bumped into the wall and
could go no further.

"Now I have you!" Coletto exclaimed, feinting to the left but
slicing to the right. Fargo, though, had pivoted, and the bowie
missed him by a cat's whisker. He lanced the Arkansas toothpick upward, going for a heart strike, but the killer pivoted and
the toothpick buried itself in Coletto's thigh instead.

Like a cat that had stepped on a hot coal, the half-breed
leaped high into the air and to one side. He landed awkwardly,
his wounded leg nearly buckling. Coletto probably thought that
by jumping beyond Fargo's reach, he had spared himself further harm. But he was mistaken.

Rather than attack, Fargo vaulted to the shotgun. It was in his
hands and he was turning when Coletto realized the mistake
he'd made and rushed forward. Fargo's thumb yanked on both
hammers. The man who had murdered Edward Webber and
countless others was almost on top of him when both barrels
went off at once.

In his wideflung travels Fargo had seen men kicked by mules
and knocked halfway to China. Once a cowboy had been sent
flying a dozen feet by a bull on a rampage. He'd witnessed men
shot by high-caliber pistols, men knocked sprawling by every

type of rifle on the frontier. But never, in all his wanderings, had Fargo seen anything to rival the impact of a double-barreled 12-gauge shotgun at close range. The results were always spectacular.

Coletto was lifted clean off his feet and thrown from the ledge as if flung by a giant hand. His barrel chest exploded, the buckshot shredding it like so much paper. For a moment he hung suspended in midair, scarlet drops cascading from him like a spring shower. Then he plummeted. Fargo darted to the edge and saw the body crash onto its spine sixty feet below. The head was driven into the cavity where the chest had been, the legs were snapped like dry tree limbs. Coletto bounced twice like a grisly ball and came to rest near the women.

The blast of the shotgun had awakened Cynthia and the others. They scrambled erect in confusion, befuddled by fatigue.

Mary Beth had Claire in her arms. Stroking the younger girl's head to calm her, she said, "It's all right now. The badman is dead. He can't hurt us." Claire wouldn't listen. Sniffling and shivering, the girl sought to break free and flee.

Fargo went over and brushed Claire's cheek with the back of his hand. She stopped struggling and looked at him. "Thank you, little one," he said.

"For what?"

"For saving my life."

Claire ran a sleeve under her nose. "I did that, Mr. Fargo? How?"

"By screaming when you did. You distracted the badman long enough for me to reach him. If not for you, I'd be dead." Fargo playfully rapped her chin with his knuckles. "You're a brave girl. I'm in your debt."

"I am?" Claire was astonished. "You are?" She wiped her nose again, and giggled. "Did you hear him, Mary? I'm brave! I saved him! Me!"

"Yes, you did," Mary said, holding her sister close. Over Claire's head she smiled gratefully, then puckered her lips and silently blew him a kiss.

Taking her elbow, Fargo steered them lower. He must move

quickly. The blast of a 12-gauge carried far, for miles if the wind was right, and at that moment it just so happened to be blowing from west to east. If Juan had sent others to find Vetch, they might hear and come to investigate. He told the women as much while climbing onto the Ovaro. "You have the shotgun, the Whitney, and now Coletto's Remington. Don't be afraid to use them if more outlaws show up."

"We'll blow their stinking heads off," Cynthia vowed. "I'll be damned if they're getting their paws on us again."

The others nodded.

Fargo wheeled the stallion but was stopped by the mention of his name.

Mary Beth and Claire had not said their good-byes. The older sibling tenderly rested her hand on his leg. "Take care. I'd hate for anything to happen to you."

"Makes two of us," Fargo quipped. The little girl reached up, wriggling her fingers, so he bent and pressed his hand over hers. "Watch out for your big sister while I'm gone. She has a knack for being caught by surprise."

Mary blushed. "I do not!"

Tittering, Claire said, "Any more badmen come, I'll save her just like I saved you. I'm not afraid."

Even Cynthia had something to say. "Come back to us, handsome. I can't tell you how nice it is to be in the company of a real man again. I'd plumb forgotten that not all men are worthless scum."

Smiling, Fargo touched his hat brim and departed. Soon the sun would set. Once it had, he'd breathe easier. The women would be safe until dawn, giving him plenty of time to do what had to be done. Provided nothing unforeseen happened. Given the odds, he had to be twenty or thirty cards shy of a full deck. No sane person would go up against Vetch's gang without help, let alone tangle with Quimico.

It was dark when Fargo drew rein at the gully where Vetch was killed. His remains were where he had left them, undisturbed, but they would not be so much longer. To the north coyotes yipped. The fresh scent of blood was luring them in for a rare feast.

Only a few lights sparkled in Paradise. Fargo circled to the north as he had done earlier, but he rode past the buildings to the cliff and then along its base until he was forty yards from the rear of the frame house. Flourishing the Colt, he cautiously approached. Lanterns lit a room on the first floor and another on the second, but there was little activity, which surprised him. Nighttime should be when Paradise came alive, when the outlaws kept the women busy for hours on end.

Dismounting, Fargo removed his spurs, stuffed them in his saddlebags, then glided to the back door. Someone had wedged it open with a chunk of wood. For the air to circulate, he figured. A hallway opened into a parlor, where he glimpsed women moving about and talking in low tones. They were upset, on edge.

Bearing to the left, Fargo stopped at the corner to scour the street. Horses were tied to the hitching posts, fifteen in all, but no one was out and about. From the saloon came gruff voices, arguing.

Fargo ran to the next building, traveling on around to the street. Checking both ways, he holstered the Colt, tucked his chin low, and ambled to the side of the saloon. A peek in the window showed that Esther wasn't there. But a lot of others were.

Juan and all of Vetch's men were on one side of the long room, Quimico and his band on the other. A palaver had been called, but neither faction trusted the other. Only Juan and Quimico were at the bar, facing one another, each with a hand hovering near his pistol. They were speaking English, which Fargo thought was strange until it hit him that many in Vetch's outfit might not know Spanish.

"—should have been back long before this," the short *pistolero* said. "Something must have happened to them."

"We will ride out at first light," Quimico said. "My men and yours will scour the countryside in all directions."

"All of us?" Juan responded. "Is that wise, with General

Diaz and his twenty *soldados* camped less than a mile to the south?"

"So?"

"So you know how he is. The pig despises us. I wouldn't put it past him to come in and steal all the women while we are gone, then blame it on you."

Quimico cursed. "Diaz would use any excuse to kill me and take my head back to Sonora. It would add to his fame. Feed his ambition to be El Presidente."

"I have told Cyrus many times that Diaz is not to be trusted," Juan said. "He always says gold coins know no boundaries. Whatever that means."

"Señor Vetch is a very smart man," Quimico remarked. "But even smart men die. Have you given any thought to what you will do?"

"Me?"

"If Vetch is dead, you are boss now. His men, this old town, the women, they are all yours."

"Mine," Juan said, wide-eyed, the enormity of it slowly sinking in.

"You will give the orders. And if you do not want to do business with Diaz, that is your right, is it not?" Quimico grinned slyly.

Fargo could guess why. With General Diaz out of the way, there was one less buyer to bid against the renegade. Fargo backed away from the window and started to cross the street. Suddenly a dusty bandit came out of the saloon, hitching at his pants, and made for the outhouse. The bandit saw him.

Stopping, Fargo let the man come closer. He plastered a friendly smile on his face while balling his right fist. *"Buenos noches. Cómo está usted?"*

Chuckling, the *bandito* pointed at his crotch and started to say something.

The moment the man lowered his eyes, Fargo smashed him on the chin. One blow was enough. The bandit toppled like a felled tree. Fargo caught him before he struck the ground, lowering the bandit quietly. Then he retraced his steps to the frame house. Mounting the pinto, he deliberately rose into the middle of the street, and galloped southward out of Paradise, making enough racket for everyone in the saloon to hear.

Fargo had a plan. By the time he was done, Cyrus Vetch's legacy would be as dead as the devious mastermind who had spawned it.

Hell was coming to Paradise.

12

The camp had been pitched in standard military formation, with two rows of tents in the center, the horses picketed under guard, and sentries patrolling the perimeter. One of them challenged Skye Fargo when he rode up, calling out in Spanish for him to halt and identify himself. Fargo responded in English, "I'm a friend of the general's, only he doesn't know it yet."

The sentry shouted toward the tents, and within a minute six more soldiers were double-timing it there, led by a beefy sergeant. Fanning out, they leveled their percussion rifles. Their uniforms were plain cloth coats and trousers, the sergeant's decorated with the insignia of his rank. He started to quiz Fargo in Spanish.

"Hold on there, mister. Do you speak English, by any chance?" Fargo felt it wiser to play the fool for a while.

"*Sí,* gringo," the sergeant said. "I speak your language. What is it you want here? We have no food to spare, if you are after a handout."

"I need to talk to General Diaz."

The noncom was immediately suspicious. "And why would you want to do that? Who are you, that the great general should give you five minutes of his precious time?"

"I have news he'll want to hear."

"Tell it to me and I will tell it to him."

"Nothing doing," Fargo said. "It's valuable. A matter of life and death, you could say. *His* life and *his* death. And if you don't let me see him, what happens to him will be on your shoulders."

The sergeant gnawed on his thick lower lip and scrutinized Fargo as he might a marauding Chiricahua. "You will leave your pinto here. You will hand your *pistola* to the sentry and be marched under guard into camp. Any sudden moves and you will be riddled with bullets. Is that clear?"

Fargo, smirking, climbed down. "I admire a man who takes his job seriously," he said, and gave the Colt to the young soldier. "Don't lose it."

Barking instructions, the sergeant had his men surround Fargo. They tramped briskly in among the tents, past several campfires, making for a tent that was much larger than the rest, with a mesh net over the front for keeping out bugs. The sergeant snapped to attention an called out in Spanish, "My apologies, my general! There is an Americano here to see you. He says it is very important."

Inside, someone stirred. The net parted and out strolled the ruler of Sonora, General Antonio Valencia Diaz. He was still in uniform, and what a uniform it was. A strutting peacock, he wore pants embroidered with gold trim and a tailored coat splashed with red and gold, as well as a red sash. He was shorter than Fargo would have thought, but his face radiated wickedness, just as the tales claimed. Giving Fargo a look of contempt, he demanded, "Who are you and what do you want?"

Fargo put on an uncertain smile. He must play his part just right or they would never take the bait. "I'm sorry to bother you. But it's worth your while to hear me out."

"I am listening," General Diaz said impatiently.

"I'm one of Vetch's men. Or I was. And I came to warn you that a trap is being laid for you."

Diaz placed his arms behind his back. "What kind of trap?"

"Well, you see—" Fargo hesitated. "I was hoping you'd find this information important enough to be worth something. Say, a hundred dollars? In gold coins? For my trouble?"

"Sergeant Canales, take this fool out and have a firing squad dispose of him," General Diaz ordered, turning on his heel. "I refuse to be trifled with."

141

"Wait!" Fargo, risking a bullet, ran around in front of the officer. "Don't you care that Cyrus Vetch is dead? Don't you care that Juan and Quimico are plotting to kill you, too?"

Sergeant Canales had drawn his pistol and was angrily advancing but the general waved him off, then regarded Fargo with renewed interest. "What is this you say? Vetch is dead? How?"

"Juan killed him. He's wanted to be top man for a long time. But he'd never have done it if Quimico hadn't talked him into it. Quimico thought Vetch was asking too much for the women. Juan has promised him a better deal."

"And you say they plot to kill me?"

"They're in the saloon right this minute, crowing about how clever they are. When I left, they were planning to put men on the roofs and behind the buildings and ambush you." Fargo held out a hand. "Is it worth the hundred?"

General Diaz had not lasted as long as he had by taking anything for granted. "Why should I trust you, Americano? What proof do you offer?"

"I couldn't very well bring Vetch's body here, now could I? But we both know I wouldn't do this if he were alive. He'd have me hunted down. And I think you know as well as I do how much Quimico hates you. He says that killing you would add to his fame. He can't wait for you to ride into his trap."

"That bastard and I have been enemies a long time," General Diaz said thoughtfully. He paced for half a minute, then came to a decision.

Fargo was ready to fight, if need be, to get away. This was the crucial moment. Had it worked? Or would Diaz have him slain?

"So they are in the saloon right now, gloating? They think to ambush *me*? The greatest general since Santa Anna?" Diaz was working himself into a rage. "This sounds like something Quimico would do! I trusted Vetch, so he uses that trust against me. Well, I'll have a surprise for him!" Diaz faced Fargo. "We will go to Paradise, you included. If everything is as you say,

142

you will have the gold coins. But if it is not as you claim, then you will die there, killed by my own hand."

Fargo grinned and said, "I wouldn't have it any other way. You'll see I'm telling the truth."

The camp was left as it was. None of the tents were struck or the fires put out. Diaz had Sergeant Canales bring Fargo to the front of the column. Several of the troopers, Fargo saw, had been instructed to carry unlit torches. They trotted northward, General Diaz dashing in a short red cap that flapped in the wind. With less than a mile to cover, they reached Paradise in minutes. Diaz signaled his men to slow to a walk when they were several hundred yards out so no one in Paradise would hear them coming. Fifty yards out they dismounted and proceeded on foot.

Fargo was relieved to find the fifteen horses still tied to the hitching posts. The street was deserted. From the saloon came loud voices.

For all his faults, General Diaz was ruthlessly efficient. He commanded his soldiers to dismount, then had them ring the saloon. The torches that had been brought were imbedded in the ground and lit, their flickering glow lighting all four sides of the dilapidated building. No one could get out without being seen.

All this had been done in the utmost silence, and now General Diaz, with Sergeant Canales on one side and Fargo on the other, walked to within a stone's throw of the entrance. "You there! Inside! I want Juan Sanchez and Quimico! This very second!"

A commotion broke out. Outlaws and *banditos* filled the doorway and spilled out, halting when they spied the ring of rifles trained on them. Quimico shoved through the crowd to the front, glaring spitefully at Diaz. "What is the meaning of this, General? Why do you come in the dark of night with your *soldados* as if to make war?"

Juan appeared and joined the renegade. More confused than angry, he said, "We didn't expect you until tomorrow, General. What can we do for you?"

"I would like to speak to Cyrus Vetch," Diaz said.

"That's not possible, I am afraid," Juan said.

"And why would that be?" the general asked.

"We think he is dead."

Diaz glanced at Fargo and said quietly, so only Fargo and Sergeant Canales heard, "You were right, Americano. They play me for a fool." Then, smiling coldly, he gazed at the outlaw and the renegade. "Did my ears deceive me? You *think* Vetch is dead? You don't *know*?"

Juan was nervous. "Cyrus has disappeared, General. There has been some trouble. The women we were holding for the auction have escaped—"

"Escaped?" General Diaz dripped scorn. "Or it is rather that you have already sold them to the cur beside you?"

"Why would I do that?" Juan responded, his nervousness rising.

From among the bandits stepped the man Fargo had slugged earlier. Excitedly, he pointed at Fargo and exclaimed, "That one! Quimico! He is the one who hit me!"

The renegade nodded knowingly, as if he understood a secret no one else did. "So the gringo is your spy, General? Don't deny it. We heard him ride out, toward your camp." Quimico dangled his arm next to his Remington. "You knew Vetch was dead before you set foot in Paradise. What game are you playing? As if I can't guess."

"Amuse me," Diaz said. "What do you think I am up to?"

"It's plain you want all the women for yourself. You sent the gringo to steal them, then had Vetch killed. Coletto also, no doubt. Now you intend to do the same to me. Later you will ride back to Mexico in triumph. I'm to be another rung on the ladder of your ambition."

General Diaz snorted. "You are loco, is what you are. You take everything you have done and twist it around to make it seem I am to blame. What else would I expect? You have always been a two-legged scorpion."

Juan Sanchez was uneasily eyeing the soldiers and the

144

torches. "I'm sure we can talk this out, General. Come into the saloon. Have a drink with us."

"And be stabbed in the back, as you must have done to Vetch?" General Diaz drew himself up to his full height and placed a hand on the revolver at his waist. "At my command!"—his voice rang out so even the soldiers at the rear would hear—"kill them all! Open *fire*!"

The troopers instantly obeyed, their first volley having a devastating effect. Eight of the outlaws dropped where they stood. Others, wounded, sought the safety of the saloon. The rest returned fire while backing indoors, their pistols flaring like giant fireflies. A cloud of gunsmoke rapidly mushroomed.

Fargo saw Juan go down, a gaping hole in his chest, the confused look on his face to the very end.

Quimico, though, was lightning fast, and had flattened when Diaz roared the order. Prone on his belly, he snapped off a shot that felled a trooper. Then he snaked to the left, under the mushrooming smoke, and Fargo lost sight of him.

It was just as well.

Fargo had his hands full simply staying alive. He crouched low, slugs whizzing on all sides and overhead. General Diaz, amazingly, stood straight as a board, fearless in his arrogance, selecting his targets carefully. Sergeant Canales had also squatted and was emptying his pistol at a knot of men in the doorway.

"My Colt!" Fargo yelled, extending his hand.

Canales brushed it aside. "When the general says so and not before." He fired again.

Fargo couldn't wait. He lowered his arm and started to turn away as if he wouldn't press the issue. But when the noncom's revolver clicked on an empty cylinder, Fargo fell onto his side as if he had been shot, then lashed out with both legs. One caught the sergeant across the chin. Canales keeled backward, stunned, offering no resistance when Fargo helped himself to his Colt.

"Tell the general he can keep his gold," Fargo said in the noncom's ear. Heaving off the ground, he ran toward the horses, zigzagging to make himself hard to hit. The soldiers and the outlaws were so engrossed in killing one another that on one tried to stop him or pick him off. Once beyond the torchlight, he ran in a straight line. He was safe, but not out of danger. Stray lead still whizzed everywhere.

None of the army mounts had run off. Swinging onto the Ovaro, Fargo scattered them by whooping like an Apache and flailing his rope. If Lady Luck smiled on him, they wouldn't stop until they reached Mexico.

Reining around, Fargo galloped to the northeast. Bedlam ruled Paradise. Guns were blasting nonstop. Men were screaming, cursing, wailing. From what Fargo could tell, the soldiers had taken cover and were picking off anyone who made a break from the saloon. Above the tempest rose General Diaz's strident voice, bellowing, "Burn them out! Torch the building!"

At the rear of the frame house, Fargo halted. The door was still ajar. He slipped noiselessly inside and down the hall to the parlor. The seven women were jammed shoulder to shoulder at the windows, watching the battle. "You could get your pretty heads blown off that way, ladies."

They whirled, scared until they saw his smile and realized he wasn't there to harm them. "Who the hell are you, big man?" asked Louise, who wore bandages around her arm where Coletto had cut her. "What do you want?"

"I only have time to say this once. I'm here to get you out. Cynthia and the others are waiting for us. I can take you to them but we must leave right away." Fargo had made it as plain as he could but there always seemed to be someone with wax in their ears.

"You're here to save us?" inquired a skinny brunette. "Then I need to fetch my bag. And my cosmetics. And the only good dress I have—"

"No!" Fargo was curt with her because it was necessary. "If you're coming, you come now. As you are. With the clothes on your back. Or stay, and spend the rest of your days being slobbered on by drunken animals. Your choice. Which will it be?" Rotating, he hurried up the hall. A glance back put him at ease.

All the women had followed, although the one who wanted her dress was pouting.

Outside, the acrid scent of smoke hung thick in the muggy air. "Do any of you know where they're keeping Esther Webber?" Fargo asked.

"That gal Quimico roughed up today?" Louise said. "Last we saw, they had her under guard in the shack across the street."

Fargo should have known. Snatching the stallion's reins, he hastened around the house toward it. The guard was gone, drawn to the battle at the end of town. Fargo didn't bother with the latch. He simply walked up and kicked the door in. Esther was bound and gagged, lying in the middle of the floor. A few strokes of the toothpick and she was in his arms, breathing her heartfelt thanks.

"We have to go," Fargo said more sternly than he intended. "Time for talk later."

Louise and Martha helped Esther stand. The women glued themselves to Fargo's heels as they moved into the open and slanted toward the stable.

Paradise was burning. The roof of the saloon was fully ablaze, great columns of smoke cascading skyward. Flames were leaping from it like blazing shooting stars, and it wouldn't be long before every last structure was engulfed in the conflagration. The buildings were so old, so dry, all it would take was a spark to set them aflame.

"Come on," Fargo goaded, running toward the wide double doors. The gunfire had reached a crescendo. The cutthroats trapped in the burning saloon were making a united effort to escape a fiery death, while the soldiers were equally determined to keep them pinned down.

"Dear God! No!" Esther suddenly cried out.

It had nothing to do with the fire. In the doorway of the stable a figure in black clothes and a red headband had materialized, leading a horse. Quimico had his Remington in his hand and raised it at the same moment Fargo raised the Colt. Neither fired.

Quimico had the women at his back. Any slug that missed him would hit one of them. He would like nothing better than to put lead into the renegade but dared not. What he couldn't understand was why Quimico didn't shoot.

"You again, hombre. Taking the women for the general?"

"I'm taking them home," Fargo answered, easing to the left.

"Home?" Quimico said. Comprehension brought a savage grin to his swarthy face. "Can it be? You're not working with Diaz, are you? You're on your own?" He laughed heartily, the Remington tilting downward. "Son of a bitch! I see it now, gringo! You've set us against one another! You used us to do what you couldn't do alone."

"I'm not done yet," Fargo said.

Quimico nodded, his dark eyes mirroring respect, and something else. "You are a man after my own heart. But it ends here. It is you and me now, hombre, and I never lose. I will kill you."

"You'll try."

The scourge of the Southwest was poised on the balls of his feet. Fargo knew Quimico would dive either to the right or the left and shoot—and he wasn't clear of the women yet. Another couple of steps should be enough, but would Quimico wait that long?

A revolver cracked. It wasn't the renegade's, though. The shot came from behind Fargo. He spun to find two *banditos* rushing out of the smoke that now choked the entire street. Springing further away from the women, Fargo stroked the trigger and the lead *bandito* pitched forward. He took another step, heard Quimico fire and the buzz of a hornet past his ear. Swiveling, he banged a round at the renegade, who was skipping back into the stable. The other *bandito* began fanning his six-shooter, but he was too far off to be accurate. Fargo showed him the error of his ways by taking steady aim and boring out the man's left eye.

The women had dropped flat, Louise urging them to stay down.

"Do as she says," Fargo directed, running toward the stable. The smoke roiled toward them like a living creature, its tendrils groping over the ground as if in search of holes to crawl into. Another couple of minutes and it would swallow them whole.

No light glowed inside. Inky murk blanketed everything. Fargo stepped into the doorway, sensed movement deeper within, and threw himself to the right. A pistol spoke, a slug thudding into the wall. Fargo answered in kind, twice, then crouched and ran to the corner where a rocking chair sat. Holding the Colt close to his stomach to muffle the sound, he replaced the spent cartridges.

Quimico would be doing the same. Now it was a war of wits, with time working in the renegade's favor. Soon smoke would flow in, filling the stable, handicapping Fargo, since he must obtain horses for the women and get the women out of there before more cutthroats showed up. He crept toward a stall.

"Are you still alive, gringo?"

The voice came from the left, toward the rear. Fargo looked for a target but saw none. He crabbed along the stall, peering between rails.

"Cat got your tongue? Or are you afraid to say?"

Fargo shifted. Quimico had changed position and was moving to the right, toward the central aisle. Fargo slowly rose to scan it.

"Got you."

The boom of the Remington was amplified by the close confines. A bullet tore into the rail under Fargo's arm, wood splinters stinging him instead of lead. A spout of flame pegged Quimico's position. Fargo snapped off two more shots, turned, and hurtled to the aisle, diving when he reached it. He landed just beyond the stall, the Colt out and the hammer back. But there was no one to shoot. Quimico wasn't there.

"Clever, hombre."

Now the killer was on the right side of the stable. Fargo scrambled onto his knees, close to the rails. He reloaded again.

Quimico said nothing else. Fargo believed the renegade was stalking him in earnest, that so far Quimico had only been trying to rattle him, to make him jumpy. A nervous man was a careless man, and a careless man was a dead one. He moved to the left, down the aisle, passing stall after stall. Thanks to the thick straw underfoot, he made little noise.

Fargo glanced toward the front. An ominous gray mass had filled the entrance, a seething ball borne by the sluggish breeze. Many of the horses became skittish, prancing and whinnying, the commotion so loud that Fargo couldn't hear Quimico if the renegade was right on top of him.

Which he was.

Fargo turned toward the rear. He stared at the end of the aisle, seeking any silhouettes that shouldn't be there. Out of the corner of his right eye he registered motion. Not in the aisle, but on the nearest stall, on the top rail. He looked up just as Quimico pounced.

In the killer's hand was a pitchfork. The tines lanced at Fargo's torso as he flung himself to the rear. He saved himself but lost the Colt when one of the tines jarred it from his grip, tearing open a finger. Blood spurting, Fargo scrabbled upright. Quimico rushed him, spearing the pitchfork.

Fargo dodged, he ducked, he weaved, and did everything he could to keep the tines from imbedding themselves. In the dark it was doubly difficult. He had only split seconds in which to react. Sooner or later he would slip up and Quimico would impale him. He couldn't keep up a pace like that forever.

Quimico was sneering, partly from confidence, partly from a sadistic urge to spill blood. He thrust low down, at Fargo's legs, then angled the pitchfork high, at Fargo's throat. By never striking twice at the same part of Fargo's body, he made it impossible for Fargo to predict what he would do next.

Stumbling, Fargo nearly had his stomach cleaved. He backed up against the front of a stall and clung to the rails to regain his balance. Quimico, taking advantage, came in fast, this time streaking the tines at his groin. Fargo wrenched aside with barely an inch to spare. He was as surprised as the renegade when the pitchfork sank into a rail with a loud *thunk*. Quimico hauled on the handle to free it but the tines were buried too deep.

Fargo charged him. The killer brought up his hands to defend himself but there was no defense against Fargo's headlong rush. Wrapping his arms around Quimico's chest, Fargo propelled his enemy across the aisle and into the opposite stall. By rights, the renegade should have had the breath knocked out of him and been easy to finish off. But Quimico was whipcord tough, wolverine vicious. He planted a fist on Fargo's jaw that rocked him backward, then knifed the flat edge of his hand across Fargo's neck. Had Fargo not been falling backward, the blow would have crushed his throat.

Quimico stabbed a hand for the Remington.

Fargo stabbed his hand for the Colt.

They were almost evenly matched. Almost. The Remington was just clearing leather when the Colt thundered once, twice, three times, and at each retort Quimico was jolted from his feet. After the last shot, the Remington slipped from fingers gone numb and the renegade slid to the ground, ending up with his back propped against a rail, his dark eyes fixed on his slayer. Quimico sucked in air.

"Who are you, gringo?"

"What difference does it make?" Fargo responded. More and more smoke was oozing into the stable and the horses were growing more and more restless. He must move swiftly.

Quimico took another deep breath. *"Por favor, hombre.* A man should know who has taken his life."

"They call me the Trailsman."

The renegade's mouth creased in a lopsided grin. "I'll be damned." He drew in the loudest breath yet, wheezed, then said, "I will speak highly of you in Hell." His hand lifted weakly in salute, and he died.

Fargo ran to the doors. The smoke was now thick enough to cut with Coletto's bowie. "Esther! Louise! Bring everyone here!"

They came, clustered like hens in a barnyard. Fargo had them stay just outside while he sped to the stalls. He gave the first five horses to the women, then he raced on down the aisle, freeing the rest. The few who balked he smacked on their rumps to get them moving. His burning lungs were craving fresh air by the time he was done. Coughing, even with a hand over his mouth and nose, he forked the Ovaro.

"I can't see!" Esther complained, swatting at the smoke.

"See, hell!" Louise declared. "I can hardly breathe! Get us out of here, handsome."

Fargo removed his rope from the saddle. Uncoiling it, he flipped the end to Louise. "Pass it along. No one is to let go until I say so." Only after every woman had a firm grip did he head westward. The smoke wrapped them in its stinging folds, making each breath torture. Burning wood crackled loudly in their ears, while to the south pistols and rifles still popped.

Seconds dragged by with awful slowness. Some of the horses were nickering and giving the women a hard time when suddenly they emerged into fresh air under a clear sky. Fargo breathed deep, then verified that everyone was accounted for. Behind them, Paradise had become a veritable inferno, a fitting end for a den of vipers.

Hoofs pounded to the west. It was Mary Beth and Claire and all the others. Not one had done as he'd told them and stayed put.

"Females," Fargo said under his breath, then grinned. What was he complaining about? By a quirk of fate, he had to escort thirteen members of the fairer sex all the way to Denver. There were worse ways to spend a week.

LOOKING FORWARD!
The following is the opening
section from the next novel in the exciting
Trailsman series from Signet:

THE TRAILSMAN #212
SIOUX STAMPEDE

*1860, Minnesota, north of the Red Lake country, where
old hatreds rose to bring new death and the only answer
was to do the wrong thing for the right reason. . . .*

Fargo groaned. The pounding that seemed like it was about to
split his head open grew worse. Lying naked, the sheet barely
covering his groin, his eyes blinked harshly as they scanned the
little room, past the large porcelain pitcher of water on the bat-
tered dresser and the faded floral hotel wallpaper. Through dry
lips, he managed a blasphemous oath. The pounding was not
just in his head, it seemed. Some of it was coming from the
door, adding insult to injury, elevating the throbbing in his temples to new heights. Rising on one elbow, he managed to find
his voice as he peered at the door.

"It's open, dammit," he rasped.

The door flew open and a figure stormed into the room. The
first thing Fargo saw was carrot red hair cut short, then a tall
form clothed in a white blouse and a denim skirt. He squinted
at a face that might have been pretty if it weren't wreathed in
frowns and drawn tight in anger. He saw her eyes move across
the muscled nakedness of his body, stopping momentarily at
his groin, then returning to his face. "You're drunk," she bit

out. "Stinking, rotten drunk." She spit the words out with a combination of shock and fury.

"Wrong," he said, his mouth feeling full of cotton. "I was drunk. And I expect to get drunk again. But I'm not right now."

"This room smells like a bourbon still," she snapped. "You're shameful, useless."

"If you say so, honey," he muttered, falling back on the bed and putting one arm over his eyes. "Now, get the hell out of here."

"I'll do nothing of the sort," Fargo heard her say.

He winced silently under his arm. "Sister, you're in the wrong place at the wrong time for the wrong reasons. Now, take off," he said.

"You're Skye Fargo, aren't you?" he heard her question.

"Last time I looked," he muttered, groaning at the now severe pounding in his head.

"Then I'm not in the wrong place. But you're a terrible disappointment," the young woman said.

Fargo took his arm away from his face and peered at her. Only her flaming red hair came to his bleary eyes clearly. "Get out, honey, whoever you are," he muttered. "Now, dammit."

"No, I'm staying right here. You're going to sober up and keep your word," she snapped.

He screwed his face up at her. "Keep my word about what?" he asked.

"You know what," she answered.

"Honey, I don't know what the hell you're talking about but I know I want you out of here," Fargo said.

"No," she threw back defiantly.

He lifted his head and winced at the pain it caused. "You ever been thrown out of a hotel room by a very angry, naked man, honey?" he asked and squinted at her.

"I've never been thrown out of a hotel room by anyone, naked or dressed," she returned indignantly.

"There's a first time for everything. You've got ten seconds to get your ass out of here on your own," Fargo said, then he fell back on the bed, closed his eyes, and cursed the incessant pounding in his brain.

"You're not getting away with this," she said threateningly and he heard her spin and start to stride away. His eyes were still closed when the pitcher of ice water hit him full in the face.

"Shit," he roared as he shuddered, and started to wrench his eyes open when the pitcher itself followed, smashing into his head. "Goddamn," he swore as new pain shot through his skull, and he felt the room spinning. He shook his head to clear it and swung his long legs from the bed. The room was still spinning, and he sat quietly for a moment as he heard the door slam shut. Shaking his head again, he pushed to his feet. "Goddamn these women," he yelled at the closed door. He muttered further curses at all redheaded females when his eyes fell upon the straight-backed chair where he'd hung his clothes. Only his clothes were no longer there, everything gone now except his boots.

Letting out an exasperated sigh, he strode for the door and stopped when he realized he was buck naked. Turning, he pulled the sheet from the bed and wrapped it around himself like a Roman toga. He then took down his gunbelt still hanging from the bedpost where he'd put it the night before, and strapped it around his waist to hold the sheet in place. Pulling on his boots, Fargo strode from the room, seeing the hallway outside was empty. Sun streaming through a hall window told him it was well into morning, and he proceeded past the front desk. The clerk, an older man in pince-nez spectacles, looked up at him. "Where'd she go?" Fargo barked.

"Out," the clerk replied. "In a hurry."

Fargo left the town's only inn, The Equity Hotel, squinting as the bright sunlight assaulted him. But anger had now pushed aside some of the throbbing in his head as he halted at a man standing by the hitching post. "Girl just left here," Fargo began, seeing the man's eyes move questioningly up and down the sheet tied around him. "Don't say it," Fargo growled. "You see her?"

"Carrot top?" the man asked.

"That's her," Fargo said.

"Rode north out of town, hell-bent for leather," the man said.

"What was she riding?" Fargo pressed.

"Big Cleveland bay, dappled hindquarters. Couldn't help noticing him. Don't see many."

"Much obliged," Fargo said and the man let his eyes move over the sheet again.

"Must've been some night," he commented gaily.

Fargo threw a harsh glare at him as he hurried down the street, ignoring the stares and hoots that followed him from the cowhands he passed. He found the general store and stepped inside. The storekeeper's eyes widened at once. "No smart-ass talk, mister," Fargo warned and silently cursed the ludicrousness of his appearance. "I want drawers, jeans, and a shirt. Everything large and hurry up."

"Yes, sir," the storekeeper said smartly, then stepped to a rack at the rear of the store and returned in moments, putting the clothes on the counter. His hand went out to rest on the apparel as Fargo reached for them. "How do you figure to pay for these, mister?" the merchant asked.

"I'll be paying for them when I get back," Fargo said.

"You got any way to prove that, stranger?" the storekeeper said.

Fargo drew his Colt. "Here's proof for now. I don't have time to argue. You'll be paid, my word on it. Now stand back, dammit," he snarled. Obeying the angry blue ice of the big man's eyes, the storekeep stepped back and watched as Fargo tossed aside the sheet and pulled on clothes that seemed to fit well enough. "I'll be back, believe me," Fargo said as he strode from the store and ran to the town stable where he'd put his horse. He saddled up the Ovaro and tossed the stableboy his saddle pouch, worth three times the stable fee. "It's yours till I get back," he said. Outside, the sun revealed the Ovaro's beauty, setting his jet black fore-and-hindquarters glistening, his pure white midsection gleaming.

Fargo sent the pinto north out of town as his eyes searched the hoofprints that crowded each other in the dry soil. He had ridden about a quarter of a mile beyond town when he was able to isolate the hoofprints he sought, the Cleveland bay's prints being wider and longer than those of most horses. He saw the prints go on for another fifty yards, then turn from the road, traveling along terrain between rows of red ash. A frown dug into Fargo's brow. There were other prints following the Cleveland bay's wide hoofmarks. They had swung in behind when the bay left the road, three sets, he noted, staying close together. The frown still creased his brow as he sent the Ovaro into a fast canter. The three sets of hoofprints stayed together, definitely following the bay as they turned suddenly between a row of thick-trunked, ancient red ash giants.

Fargo caught sight of a small pond sparkling in the sun directly ahead when he heard the short scream, a voice he remembered very well. "Let go of me!" he heard, followed by a sharp gasp of pain. Fargo pulled the pinto to a halt and swung from the saddle. Dropping into a crouch, he silently ran forward, seeing the figures take shape in a small clearing by the pond. Once more, the carrot red crop of hair caught his eye before anything else. Three men came into sight, one holding the young woman, pinning her arms behind her. He noted their three horses together, the Cleveland bay beside a flat rock at the edge of the pond. Fargo crept to the edge of the trees, dropping to one knee. The man holding the young woman had a pudgy-cheeked, baby face that didn't seem to match the thin cruelty of his lips.

"Damn you," the woman said and brought her shoe down hard on the man's ankle. He roared in pain, his grip loosening, allowing the young woman to pull away. She turned to run when one of the others brought her to the ground with a flying tackle. He held her down as the baby-faced one rose and hit her across the face with the back of his hand.

"Goddamn little bitch," he swore and yanked her to her feet as the other one kept hold of her arms. The third man, a thin, sharp-nosed figure with stringy black hair, stepped forward.

"Real little piece of dynamite, isn't she?" he cackled lecherously.

"Yeah. She'll shore be fun to screw," the baby-faced one said.

"Me first," the angular one cut in.

"Why you?" the third man asked.

"I'm the one whose idea it was to follow her to town," the sharp-nosed one said.

"What about getting rid of her?" the third one asked.

"No reason we can't enjoy ourselves, first," the pudgy-cheeked one replied, reaching out and grabbing the girl's calves, pulling her legs out from under her as she went down. The third man kept her arms pinned tightly behind her. "You can go next," he growled and fell to his knees, looming over the girl.

"Rotten, stinking bastards!" the young woman bit out, turning and twisting her torso as she kicked out with both legs.

"Hold her still, dammit," the baby-faced one snapped as he lowered himself over the young woman, and began to push her skirt up. Fargo drew the big Colt. Putting a bullet into the one half atop her would be easy enough, but his finger stayed poised against the trigger. Sure, it would be easy, but still very risky. The bullet from the powerful Colt could go right through him and into the young woman beneath him. Fargo grimaced, rose to his feet, and stepped into the open.

"That'll be all, mister," he growled, seeing the three men freeze in place for a moment. The sharp-nosed one turned first, spinning to face the voice and starting to reach for his gun. "Wouldn't try that," Fargo said calmly. The man eyed the Colt leveled at him, then let his hand drop to his side. But his eyes told Fargo he was waiting for a better moment. "Get off her," Fargo said to the baby-faced one still leaning over the girl. The man pushed himself up, and thought about going for his gun when he saw the Colt shift a fraction of an inch to point at his chest.

"Who the hell are you?" he blurted.

"That's no matter to you," Fargo said.

"You know her?" the man asked.

"In a way," Fargo said, his eyes flicking to the young woman, seeing the mixture of hope and fear on her face as the third man still held on to her.

"You've got two seconds to get out of here alive," the baby-faced one said.

"Can't do that," Fargo replied evenly.

Pudgy cheeks lifted his head in disbelief. "You some kind of crazy? You figure to take on all three of us?" the man said.

Fargo smiled. "Like sitting ducks," he said. "You boys have only one thing to decide: who gets shot first." He saw the three exchange quick, uneasy glances, keeping the calm smile on his lips. Fargo had already won the first round. He'd made them suddenly unsure of themselves, uncertain of the man they faced. If they drew on him, they'd do so nervously, jerkiness replacing smooth motion. He knew he could outdraw any one of them, but still he'd added precious split seconds to his advantage. They continued to hesitate, and Fargo noted the baby-faced man's fingers twitching. "You want to let her go now?" Fargo said quietly. "I'm a man with a short fuse."

"You're a man with a short life," the sharp-nosed one threw back, but there was only nervous bravado in his voice.

"Your call," Fargo said, shifting the Colt for emphasis, when the third one still holding on to the girl proved he was the smartest of the trio.

"Pull that trigger and she gets it," he called. Fargo flicked his glance at him and cursed silently. The man had drawn his gun, and now had it pushed into the young woman's ribs. In a flash, everything had changed, Fargo realized. His advantage had vanished. It had all become a new and deadly game. But he knew one thing. He had to play it out. He couldn't let them think they had seized the upper hand or the carrot-topped woman was finished. He let his eyes bore into the man holding her, lifting his shoulders in a shrug.

"You do your thing. I'll do mine," Fargo said and saw surprise come into the man's eyes.

"Thought she was a friend of yours," the man said.

"Not exactly," Fargo said.

"Then what the hell are you doin' here?" the baby-faced one broke in.

"She has something of mine I want back. I don't much care if she's dead or alive so long as I get it," Fargo said steadily as he drew the hammer back on the Colt. "You can get yourselves killed with her or not." He waited as his stomach churned. Fargo was playing the bluff to the end, and he was afraid one of them would do the wrong thing and the standoff would burst out of control. And it was the girl who would pay the price. He grew more certain that that was going to happen with every passing second. The one with the gun in her ribs had become the key player, the most dangerous of all of them, now. His head and shoulders were in the open behind the redhead, whose eyes now showed only fear and desperation.

Fargo drew a deep breath. He knew only someone with his marksmanship, and the accuracy of a Colt, had a chance at making the shot. But he had no choice. He couldn't take the two in front of him, first. It would trigger the man holding the girl into firing, and that was the first thing he was trying to prevent. Fargo glanced at the man, drawing a mental bead on his target, allowing himself another split second before pressing the trigger. He had time only to see the man's skull explode in a shower of red and hear the girl scream, and then he was diving, catapulting himself to the ground and rolling away from where he stood.

He heard the volley of shots from the other two as they drew and fired, feeling some of the bullets whizzing past him. But, as he had expected, they fired too quickly and unevenly. Fargo was now in the trees, rolling onto his stomach on a bed of lance-shaped smartweed as he saw the sharp-nosed man turn to fire at the girl. The Colt barked out two shots that almost blended together as one, and the man staggered, spun, and collapsed. Fargo's lake blue eyes turned away, seeking out the third man, and found the baby-faced figure had already reached the horses. "Hold it right there and you can see tomorrow," Fargo called. The man paused, one hand on the saddle horn of his horse, then turned to fire a volley of shots into the trees where Fargo's voice had echoed. Two of the bullets dug into the ground inches from his elbow as he steadied the Colt.

The man had swung onto his horse when Fargo fired. The horse rose up, its forefeet flailing the air as its rider fell backward over its rump. The man hit the ground and lay still. "Damned fool," Fargo muttered, holstering the Colt as he rose, then stepped from the trees and walked toward the young woman as she pushed to her feet. Her dark azure eyes leveled at him as he reached her, her lips parted, her words coated with awe. "It all happened so fast," she stammered.

"That's usually the way," Fargo said.

Her eyes continued to peer hard at him. "Thank you," she managed to say.

He grunted in reply. "Wait here," he said and went to where the baby-faced man lay beside the horses. He knelt down, went through the man's pockets, and found nothing to identify him. His saddlebag held nothing either, and Fargo quickly checked the other two with the same results. But he found himself frowning as a strange odor sifted into his nostrils. Turning, he followed his nose, finding the aroma leading to the horses. The odor grew stronger, much of it coming from their hooves, pasterns, and ankles. *Must have been something they had walked in,* he thought, frowning, and drew the odor into his nostrils again. It was a dark smell, dank and slightly moldy, with a sharp pungency to it. He'd smelled it before, he reckoned, not often, but enough to remember. But he still couldn't put a name to it. Setting it aside in his mind, he returned to where the young woman waited and had the first opportunity to really look at her without bourbon or sixguns in his way.

The carrot red hair, though cut short, tumbled with its own fullness over an even-featured face with thin eyebrows atop her dark blue eyes. She had a straight, aquiline nose and lips that were nicely shaped, while not really full. She had the kind of milky white skin that so often went with orange-red hair. His eyes took in her tall, slender figure, the white shirt resting on longish breasts perhaps a little shallow at the tops, but nicely filled out below. Lean hips drew into long legs that tapered nicely under the skirt. As he took her in, he saw the coolness return to her eyes.

"It seems you can be competent when you're sober," she said.

"Competent? Is that all I was?" he snapped.

She let the coolness leave her eyes. "All right, a lot more than competent, I'll concede," she said.

"Damn right you will." Fargo grunted, peering at her. "Being nice is hard for you, isn't it?"

"Sometimes, especially when I'm given good reason not to be," she returned, bristling at once.

"I've come for my clothes," he stated gruffly. She turned, went over to the big bay, took Fargo's things from the saddlebag, and handed them to him.

"I was going to return them," she said tartly. "I didn't expect you'd be able to follow me."

"Aren't you lucky I was," Fargo said as her face softened, her cool good looks suddenly giving way to warm prettiness.

"Yes, I'm grateful for that. Really, I am," she said.

"You should be," he growled, his anger at her returning. "You know why those three came after you?"

162

She shrugged. "A woman riding alone. Easy pickings. That kind doesn't need more of a reason."

"Guess not," Fargo said.

"But you're thinking something else," she said, picking up on his tone quickly.

"Just wondering about the way they said things. One talked about getting rid of you as if that was first on their minds. Another said there was no reason they couldn't enjoy themselves, first," Fargo said.

She thought for a moment. "I didn't know them, never saw them before. I'd guess that was just their way of talking."

"You're probably right," he agreed. "You've a name?"

"Amity," she said. "Amity Baker."

"Amity," he repeated. "That sure as hell doesn't fit."

"Not when I'm cheated out of hard-earned money. Not when people get roaring drunk instead of keeping their word," she snapped.

He stepped back, took in the indignation in her face that held a lacing of disappointment with it. "Honey, you've got three minutes to tell me what the hell this is all about. Start talking fast," he said.

"Not here," she said, glancing at the three figures on the ground, a tiny shudder coursing through her. Turning, she pulled herself onto the Cleveland bay, mounting with a lithe, smooth motion that didn't even give sway to her breasts. He climbed onto the Ovaro and rode beside her as she went around to the other side of the pond, away from the three corpses, before she stopped. He slid to the ground with her. "You're a strange man, Fargo," she said, more perplexity than anger in her voice.

"That's been said before," he remarked dryly.

"You keep insisting you don't know why I came looking for you, yet you risked your life to save me," Amity Baker said.

"Call the last one a good deed. I don't know a damn thing about the first," Fargo said.

163

"You going to tell me you don't know Rufe Thomson?" Amity challenged, putting her hands on her slender hips.

Fargo's eyes narrowed at her with sudden caution. "No, I'm not going to tell you that," he said carefully.

"Good. Then you'll admit that he acts as an agent for you," she said.

Fargo felt the caution growing inside him. "From time to time," he said. "We go back a long ways, Rufe and I."

She reached into her skirt pocket, brought out a square of paper, and thrust it at him. He recognized Rufe's handwriting on it at once. "You going to try and deny that?" Amity flung at him. Fargo began to read the square of paper, already feeling the furrow cross his brow.

This will spell out the agreement between Miss Amity Baker of Green Hills, Minnesota, and Mr. Skye Fargo, generally known as the Trailsman, wherein Skye Fargo agrees, for the sum of one thousand dollars cash paid herewith, to break trail for the herd owned by Amity Baker.

Signed hereby for Skye Fargo by Rufe Thomson on this day of July 18, 1860.

Fargo noted Rufe's scrawling signature that followed, his frown now deeper on his brow as he handed the paper back.

"Well?" Amity demanded imperiously.

"Sometimes Rufe overstepps himself," Fargo began. "He knew I'd just finished a job and was on my way to visit. You put down a powerful lot of money. I'd say he got carried away and tried to make everybody happy."

"When he wrote out this agreement he told me when to come back. I did, and somebody in his office directed me to your room. I found you hardly fit to fulfill your commitment," Amity said reproachfully.

"I didn't make a commitment," Fargo said.

"Rufe Thomson made it for you," she countered.

164

"Rufe had no power to make it."

"You admitted he acted as an agent for you."

"I said he had from time to time, all on his own. He never had any right to. I just went along those other times," Fargo said.

"I'd like to hear what Rufe Thomson has to say about that," she snapped.

"Rufe's dead," Fargo said quietly, seeing Amity Baker's eyes grow wide and her lips drop open in shock.

"Oh, my. Oh, oh my," she breathed. "I'm sorry."

"Didn't know it myself till I rode in the day after it happened. He was killed in a holdup robbery in his office," Fargo said. "That's why I was in bed with a bottle of bourbon. Figured it'd help deal with the memories. As I said, Rufe and I went back a long time."

"I'm sorry. I had no idea. They just sent me back to the hotel room. I didn't know," Amity said.

"Now you do. I'm going back to finish remembering," Fargo said.

"You mean finish drinking," she said with instant reproach.

He shrugged. "A toast to remember, another to forget, and a couple to ask why. That's the way of it."

"You can't just walk away. I need your help. And I have an agreement," she protested.

"With a dead man who was wrong to make it in the first place. Sorry, honey," Fargo said and pulled himself onto the pinto.

"This isn't fair," she threw back angrily.

He paused, fastening her with a penetrating stare. "Fair? Who told you life was fair?" he said. "Ask Rufe about fair." He started to turn the pinto.

"Dammit, Fargo. I need you," she pleaded, and he saw the redheaded temper exploding inside her again. "You're being rotten."

"Think of those three varmints and say that again," he told

her softly. Her curvaceous lips tightened and he saw remorse fighting with her temper.

"Go away," she murmured almost in a whisper.

"Amity's a nice name. Try living by it," he tossed back as he sent the pinto into a canter, feeling her eyes stay on him as he circled the pond and headed back to town. He kept a steady pace and found himself wondering if he'd seen the last of that carrot red hair.